THE KINGDOM SERIES

BOOK 1

# KINGDOM'S DAWN

## CHUCK BLACK

MULTNOMAH

KINGDOM'S DAWN

© 2001, 2006 by Chuck Black

Published in association with The Steve Laube Agency, LLC
5501 North Seventh Avenue #502, Phoenix, AZ 85013

International Standard Book Number: 978-1-59052-679-8

Interior illustrations by Marcella Johnson
"Expedition" music © 2002 by Emily Elizabeth Black;
lyrics © 2002 by Chuck Black
Interior design and typeset by Katherine Lloyd, The DESK
Unless otherwise indicated, Scripture quotations are from:
*The Holy Bible,* New King James Version
© 1984 by Thomas Nelson, Inc.

Published in the United States by Multnomah,
an imprint of the Crown Publishing Group,
a division of Penguin Random House LLC, New York.

MULTNOMAH® and its mountain colophon are registered trademarks
of Penguin Random House LLC.

Printed in the United States of America

Library of Congress Cataloging-in-Publication Data
Black, Chuck.
Kingdom's dawn / Chuck Black.
    p. cm. -- (The kingdom series ; bk. 1)
ISBN 1-59052-679-1
I. Title.
PS3602.L264K557 2006
813'.6--dc22

                                                      2006005686

"A *Pilgrim's Progress* for the Xbox generation! That's what Chuck Black has achieved in his Kingdom Series, an allegory of the whole Bible told in a medieval format of noble knights and scathing sword fights, quests and dragons, betrayal and final victory by the true Prince over the Dark Knight."

—DAVE JACKSON
author of the *Trailblazer* novels

"Take up the sword handed to you and boldly carry it through the pages of Chuck Black's Kingdom Series. You'll be held captive by a creative journey through a distant world that leads to God's Word…and a kingdom like no other."

—TIM WESEMANN
author of *Swashbuckling Faith:*
*Exploring for Treasure with Pirates of the Caribbean*

*To my father and mother, Jim and Frances.*

Your love, instruction, and encouragement
inspired me,
but most importantly,
you showed me the light and led me to Him.
Thank you!

# CONTENTS

Prologue: VOYAGE TO THE EDGE .............. 9

Chapter 1: VISION SEARCH ................... 12

Chapter 2: THE SERVANT'S SWORD ............ 19

Chapter 3: A KINGDOM LOST ................ 29

Chapter 4: YESTERDAY'S END ................ 44

Chapter 5: A SWORD AND A MISSION ......... 60

Chapter 6: LET THEM HEAR .................. 69

Chapter 7: NO PLACE A HOME ............... 80

Chapter 8: BETRAYED! ....................... 90

Chapter 9: BEGINNING OF BONDAGE .......... 97

Chapter 10: MASTERY UNVEILED ............. 102

Chapter 11: A SAVAGE BATTLE .............. 115

Chapter 12: JOURNEY TO DEATH ............. 123

Chapter 13: STORM OF SALVATION ........... 129

Chapter 14: A QUESTION OF FAITH .......... 137

Epilogue: AT KINGDOM'S EDGE .............. 145

Discussion Questions ......................... 146

Answers to Discussion Questions ............... 152

"Expedition": Written for *Kingdom's Dawn* ......... 156

Author's Commentary .......................... 158

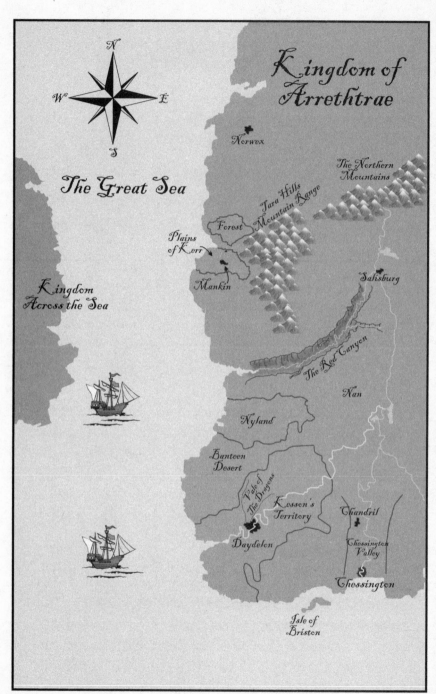

© Chuck Black

# VOYAGE TO
# THE EDGE

 The occasional cool mist of the sea quietly reminds me of the unyielding truth of my journey. I am too far from battle to feel the rush within my muscles and yet too close to sleep.

The ship I am on is a grand ship and is only one of many. The night breeze chills my moist face as I gaze across the rhythmic mass and see the outline of hundreds of other gallant ships. Gallant ships carrying gallant knights. As I lean upon the mast, the creak of the timber and the melodic swish of each wave breaking against the bow tug upon my memories.

I am Cedric...Cedric of Chessington. You and I are alike in that we are on a journey. I am not referring to my trek upon this ship, although it is the final leg of my journey. No, my journey began a long time ago, when I was just a boy.

At ten years old, my heart was full of dreams and adventure. An old man by the name of Leinad enticed my appetite for adventure with his stories. His impact on my life was powerful, though I did not realize it at the time. I believed him as a boy, humored him as a young man, and honor him now, for the stories he told of his life were true. They were of a truth that lost its believability as I grew into the reality of life and dared not believe. And yet, here I am on an adventure every bit as unbelievable as Leinad's.

As I close my eyes, the moist air reminds me of the damp smell of spring nearly twenty-five years ago. There was a small stream east of Chessington that meandered south until it emptied into the vast sea. I loved to play upon its banks with my friend William. Our swords of willow clicked in the morning sunlight as we rescued the fair lady from the clutches of the Dark Knight.

William had been warned by his parents to stay away from the "crazy old man" who lived in a hut near the river, but I could not. He was odd for sure, but he was not dangerous at all. His tales of valor drew me to him. He was a mentor and a friend, and the memory of his voice has been a companion to me often, especially now that I know how his life fits so perfectly into the King's plan for the kingdom. He had the voice of a seasoned knight...

"Sit down, lad, and share a slice of apple," Leinad said as my mouth became wet in anticipation of the tart fruit. His worn hands worked the knife firmly and delicately to produce eight perfect slices.

"Sir Leinad, please tell me again about the mighty sword," I pleaded as he slid a cracked wooden bowl across the table with the green apple slices. I thanked him and took a small nibble of my first slice to allow my mouth a chance to recover from the blast of sweetness that flooded my tongue and cheeks.

His silver hair seemed to betray the heart of a mighty warrior within. Though he was old, his shoulders were broad and his arms were strong. The firewood he chopped was an easy challenge for him, and the blade of the ax landed on its target every time. His gentle brown eyes were framed by tan wrinkles that ran toward his temples. They were eyes that I could gaze into and not turn away from. At times during his orations they became a living canvas that revealed love, pain, courage, and fear. The years of age only slightly masked what I knew was once a very handsome young man.

"Ah, Cedric, my dear boy," he said and lowered himself into an adjacent chair on my right. It faced him toward a window that looked south to the sea, which was just beyond one's vision. "That is a story worth its telling."

A veteran hand landed on my shoulder, and his smile accompanied a wink. "It was a new beginning for the people, the dawn of a new kingdom…"

Leinad's story is one of knights, swords, treachery, and love. There is no story like it, and though it is my beginning, it is his story—a story that must not be forgotten.

## CHAPTER ONE

# VISION SEARCH

 The razor-sharp tip of the sword screamed deathly close to Leinad's chest as he quickly recovered from a foolish overextended thrust aimed for his opponent's torso.

*I'll never underestimate his speed again,* thought Leinad as he carefully took up his position, once again facing the older man. A quick exchange of cuts and parries ensued with no clear advantage. The older man advanced an attack with seasoned experience, carefully but aggressively. Leinad countered each attack with precision and confidence as he gave slightly, waiting for the expended energy to take its toll on the muscled frame of the older man. At sixteen years old, Leinad was just a boy to some, but his daily training by his mentor had developed strength and discipline in him before his time.

There it was—the first hesitation in his opponent's volley of cuts was a clear indication to Leinad that his attack was ending. He had studied his opponent carefully and knew that if he was to be victorious, he had to capitalize on such a moment as this. As he deflected the last cut to his left, Leinad quickly rotated his body one full circle, which doubled the force of his blade as it raced toward the older man's stomach. He risked the momentary unprotected exposure of his back based on the fatigue he sensed in his opponent. If he miscalculated, he would die. If he was successful, he would be the victor.

As he neared completion of the circling maneuver, Leinad turned his head to locate the target for his following sword to strike, sure that it was impossible for the older man to retreat quickly enough to avoid his deadly blow. He was suddenly gripped with fear. His sword was screaming toward nothing but air; his opponent was gone.

The older man had dropped to one knee and raised his sword for protection as he saw the deadly arc of Leinad's sword coming toward him. Leinad knew in an instant that he had miscalculated once again.

"Observation and experience build prediction, for if you study the past, you will know the future." Leinad recalled this lesson from his mentor, and now he was about to die as a consequence of forgetting it.

The speed of the sword was too great for him to change its direction, and yet once the sword passed over the head of his adversary, he would never be able to recover in time to stop the fatal thrust from his opponent that would surely follow. As the sword approached the vacant target just above the head of the master swordsman, Leinad pulled and jumped with all his might, using the momentum of the sword to catapult him, as though he were mounting a horse, over the top of the older man.

The last-chance maneuver sent Leinad tumbling on the ground behind the older man, but he was able to regain his footing before his opponent could turn and attack again.

The two swordsmen faced each other once again with sweat-soaked tunics and brows that could no longer hold the salty fluid that fell from their foreheads. The lush green meadow that hosted this fight seemed to wait patiently for its interrupted peace to return. The fight had lasted much longer than either of them had experienced before, and there was still no sign of a champion.

Leinad looked into the eyes of the older man—eyes that revealed experience, wisdom, and patience. He sensed a mutual respect for each other's skill as a swordsman and for each other's character as a man.

"That was a bit daring, son!" Leinad's father said as he yielded his sword to his scabbard.

Leinad smiled and knew that his father had just rebuked him for his carelessness.

"I'm sorry, Father. I will be more careful in the future," Leinad said as he too found a home for his sword in his own scabbard.

Leinad had been trained by his father every day for the past four years in the art of the sword. Peyton was a master swordsman, and Leinad saw his father's commitment to pass this mastery on to him through these lessons. Leinad also learned from his father that sword training alone was more devastating than helpful to a young man were it not tempered with discipline, honor, integrity, loyalty, and honesty—the very qualities his father demonstrated each day. Today Leinad revealed his proficiency, and he knew he was fast becoming a master swordsman like his father.

Leinad was of average height but still growing. With dark hair that curled when wet, he bore a strong resemblance to his father, which even included the slight dimple in his chin. His smile was slightly higher on the left and accentuated the handsome features of a maturing young man. He felt himself growing stronger each day, but he knew his boyish look was still quite evident. Leinad was glad that his voice no longer cracked when he talked. He found it difficult to say the right things to folks other than his father, and attempting conversation with a voice that cracked didn't help matters. Leinad's eyes were different than Peyton's though, for the deep, sharp eyes of his father gave way to the compassionate eyes of his mother.

Leinad remembered his mother, although the image of her delicate face had become faint with the passing years. This upset Leinad, and he clung to the memory of her love for him all the more. Dinan had died when Leinad was eight. Even then Leinad could sense a deep ache in her heart that never seemed to leave her. The winter she fell sick and died was too grievous a time for Leinad to talk about. He assumed that was true for his father as well since he talked only of the pleasant times they once had as a family.

Although it was not complete, his father's gentle love was enough to carry Leinad into manhood without his mother. His father fulfilled both roles as well as any man could. Leinad knew this and responded with respect and loyalty.

As they walked toward a favorite sprawling oak tree for

a time of recovery, Peyton placed his arm around Leinad's shoulder.

"Excellent lesson today, son. After our rest, how about we clean up and make a trip to town for some supplies?"

Leinad looked up slightly to meet his father's eyes, for he was nearly equal in height, and smiled. Any time there was a break in the routine labor of the farm, Leinad enjoyed it. At first that was why he loved the lessons in sword fighting. But later he came to love the training because he had reached a point where he knew he was quite competent with the sword. Although he knew he was far from his father's level of mastery, Leinad loved the fact that he was a challenge to him. For a long time he ignored the question that never left his mind: *What does sword fighting have to do with farming?*

The young lad loved to be in the presence of his father. There he felt secure. Not that Leinad ever felt threatened, for all he had ever known since he could remember was a peaceful life in the land. Unlike many youths of sixteen, Leinad never saw his father as an overbearing fool. He could see the depth of wisdom that resided in his father, and he never questioned the truth and sincerity of his love for him.

Peyton was a tall man with a well-seasoned muscular frame. His dark hair was accompanied by wisps of gray near his temples, and his eyes were deep and sharp but not harsh. His hands were large and leathery from long hours of working the land. Early on Leinad knew that his father's hands were fashioned for a different purpose—they had not always been the hands of a farmer. It was in the last four years that this was made obvious to him since his father had begun teaching Leinad skills quite different from those required to grow food from the land.

After each had taken long drinks from their water flasks, they dug into a knapsack and enjoyed the sweet taste of fresh fruit. Now that peace had returned to the meadow, so had the songs of the birds.

Leinad and his father lived in the Plains of Kerr, which was along the western shore of the kingdom. The Great Sea bordered the kingdom on the west and down to the south as well. Most of the inhabitants of the Plains of Kerr were farmers. The town of Mankin served as a central community for the people as well as a place of trade for travelers from other regions of the kingdom.

Leinad's farm was a half-day's walk north of Mankin, and the Great Sea was just as far to the west. It was lush, beautiful country. The farm rested on the northern edge of the Plains of Kerr. Rugged wilderness and forested country filled with wildlife was north of the farm, which afforded Leinad and his father many days of excellent hunting. Just to the east of the farm was the gentle meadow in which their lessons of the sword usually took place. It was in this meadow that they now were enjoying a moment of rest.

"Your sword skills have greatly improved, Leinad," Peyton said. "Do not become impatient with the fight. Impatience breeds recklessness, and recklessness will end in defeat against a skilled opponent. It is the patient perfecting of the fundamentals that wins battles. That is why I have worked with you to improve your strength and focus your mind, but you must decide that you will discipline yourself to use them."

"I understand," Leinad said. "Father, may I ask you a question?"

"Certainly."

"What does sword fighting have to do with farming?"

Peyton finished a draw on his flask and wiped his mouth with the back of his hand. "No matter what a man's occupation, he must be ready to fight for the King. One never knows if he will be called upon to serve the King in battle."

Peyton paused and looked at Leinad. "But honestly, son, for you it will mean much, much more." He did not wait for the next inevitable question. "Come. Let's clean up and get to town so we can return home before dark."

## CHAPTER TWO

# THE SERVANT'S SWORD

Peyton and Leinad entered the outskirts of Mankin midafternoon on their horses. The streets were moving with their usual activity. Mankin had no protective walls surrounding it and thus was vulnerable to raids from various bands of marauders. It was the crafty and sometimes less-than-honorable town prefect who actually kept the community thriving in spite of these bands of thieves. When necessary, he paid off the marauders with a portion of the duty he collected from the inhabitants of the town. The payoff might be gold coins, food, or weapons. The thieves never went so far as to hinder the town's potential to recover and provide another payoff. When possible, the bell in the tower located at the town square was sounded to warn the people. A short burst of clangs called a town meeting, but a continuous ringing of the bell meant the marauders were on their way. This allowed parents time to gather their children off the streets, for it was not unusual for a stray youngster to end up as a slave in a distant land.

After buying some cooking supplies at the town market, Peyton and Leinad walked their horses toward the blacksmith's shop at the end of the main thoroughfare.

"I need Gabrik to fix a shoe on Rosie here," Peyton said as they passed by various shops in the town. Leinad noticed that any time they came to town, his father always found an opportunity to stop at the blacksmith's shop. There was an unusual bond between his father and Gabrik. Leinad could never quite understand why there was any friendship at all since Gabrik was stern and spoke very little. Although his work was superb, the townsfolk entered his shop only for business. Both Gabrik and the townsfolk were content with their business-only relationship.

"Gabrik is an awfully serious fellow, Father," Leinad said as they neared the shop. "What's his story?"

"Why don't you ask him?" Peyton said with a slight smile.

"Are you kidding? The man is huge! I'll not risk upsetting him. Besides, every time we go to his shop, he stares at me as though I need watching."

Peyton laughed. "Trust me, Leinad, you have never seen Gabrik upset. And as for his demeanor toward you, I think he likes you."

Leinad stifled his own laugh and thought privately how glad he was that their encounters with Gabrik were brief and infrequent.

The familiar sound of hot steel being pounded into a usable form met his ears. Leinad tied his horse to the hitching post, and Peyton led his horse to the open door of the shop, where a large, dark-skinned man looked up from his work.

"Gabrik, my friend…greetings!" Peyton smiled and raised a friendly hand.

Gabrik's countenance softened slightly when he saw Peyton. He nodded his greeting and doused his work in the cooling tank. Hissing white steam rose into the air around Gabrik, and the hammer came to rest on his anvil.

"Hello, Peyton." His voice was deep and slightly accented. It was an accent that matched none other that Leinad had ever heard. Gabrik wiped the sweat from his brow and some soot from his hands with a cloth. That unsettling stare once again came to rest on Leinad.

Every time Leinad saw Gabrik, he was amazed at his size. He stood a full head taller than Peyton, and his sweat-soaked tunic did little to hide the massive muscles beneath it. His jet-black hair was short and straight. His eyes were a hazel-green mix and were set deep. Leinad could not force himself to look into those penetrating eyes for more than a brief moment.

He met Gabrik's gaze and then found a sword to study hanging on a nearby wall. Gabrik's finest work was in the swords he made. The work was of such quality that Leinad wondered why he was blacksmithing in a region of the kingdom where there was more need for plows and horseshoes than for swords. And yet, for as long as Leinad could remember, Gabrik had been the community blacksmith and swordsmith.

"What can I do for you today, Peyton?" Gabrik asked.

"Rosie needs a shoe repaired," Peyton said.

Gabrik immediately went to work, and the shoe was fixed in short order.

"Gabrik, how is your other work coming along?"

Gabrik glanced toward Leinad. "I finished it two days ago. Would you like to see it?"

"Yes, I believe I would," Peyton said.

Gabrik walked to the back of his shop, through a door, and into his storage room. When he returned, he was carrying an item wrapped in cloth. He set it before Peyton and Leinad on a wooden worktable.

Gabrik opened the cloth to reveal a beautiful, masterfully crafted sword. It surpassed the splendor of even Peyton's sword. Leinad's jaw dropped slightly as his eyes scanned every detail of the magnificent sword. He yearned to hold it, but his temperance forbade him. The blade was razor sharp and shined like white silver. From the hilt to midway up the blade was an ornate and intricate inlaid pattern. The handle was gold with more intricate design on the guard. The pommel contained the distinct insignia of the King, just as Peyton's sword did.

"It is absolutely splendid, Gabrik!" Peyton said as he too admired the fine work.

"The steel in the blade was folded over two hundred times," Gabrik said without emotion or pride.

Leinad became aware of his gawk and tried to show mature restraint instead. "Who is it for?" he asked Gabrik. It was the first question Leinad had ever asked him, and it brought another gaze from

Gabrik that made Leinad wish he had stayed silent.

"I do believe this is the finest sword in all of Arrethtrae," Peyton said, seemingly unaware that Leinad had spoken.

Gabrik looked back at Peyton. "Only one sword surpasses it," he said matter-of-factly.

"Yes," said Peyton, "and I was fortunate enough to see that one as well. There has never been, nor will there ever be, a sword that equals that of the King!"

Gabrik nodded. "True indeed, true indeed."

Gabrik covered the sword once again with the cloth. "The scabbard is also nearly finished. Within the next day or so, my work will be done." He left the room to return the sword to its place of rest.

Upon Gabrik's return, Peyton thanked him and paid for the work done on Rosie's shoe. They exchanged parting courtesies and turned to leave the shop. Leinad followed his father outside, and as he neared the threshold, he heard Gabrik's bass voice.

"Leinad." It was the first time he had spoken directly to the boy.

Leinad turned and felt his cheeks flush slightly, not knowing what verbal retribution would be added to the soul-penetrating stares he always received.

"The sword is for one who is willing to serve the King...and the people."

For a moment, Gabrik's eyes did not cut Leinad as they had so often in the past—they searched. Leinad hesitated, nodded his appreciation, and turned to leave.

Down the street, Peyton and Leinad stopped at a shop to purchase some fresh bread, fruits, vegetables, and venison to add some variety to their food pantry on the farm. Soon they would bring a portion of their own produce to town to sell and trade.

As they exited the shop, Leinad glanced up the street and missed a rise in the threshold, which nearly sent him to the cobblestoned pavement. The sack of food spilled onto the ground, and an apple rolled four paces to the dirty feet of a young girl who looked every bit a street orphan. Leinad quickly recovered his balance and his dignity and began to restock his bag. He kept one eye on the girl, fully expecting her to grab the fruit and bolt. Her hair was a gnarled mess, and its color was undistinguishable, although Leinad thought it might be reddish. She wore a tattered dress that was as plain as the dirt on the street. The thin cloth hung limply on her lean body. Her cheeks were soiled, but her eyes were not empty as one might expect. The spark of life was still evident in those bright blue eyes.

Leinad turned away from the girl to finish filling the sack and to provide an opportunity for the girl to escape with her booty unnoticed. He knew his father would have given the hungry girl some food anyway as he had done for many others in the past. Figuring enough time had elapsed, he turned back and nearly dropped the bag again. The girl was standing directly in front of him with her arm outstretched, apple in hand. Leinad gazed at her somewhat surprised and perplexed.

"If you's goin' ta give me the food, you needs ta say so 'cause I don't like pretendin' I's stealin'," the young girl said in a matter-of-fact way.

"It's okay," Leinad said. "You can have it."

"Thanks, mister!"

Peyton joined the two. "What's your name, missy?" he asked.

"Name's Tess. But it don't really matter none 'cause nobody knows it or cares much." Her voice dropped slightly.

Leinad felt guilty for his own good life as he looked at the pathetic form of this young girl. She looked three or four years younger than he. He figured the odds were she had never seen a meal as good as he ate three times a day.

"That's not true, Tess," Peyton said. "A person's name always matters, no matter who you are. And there are people who care. You just don't know it yet. Tell me, where are your parents?"

Tess thought for a moment. It looked to Leinad as though she was trying to remember if she'd ever had parents. "I ain't got no parents. They was killed when I was little." The words were rather emotionless.

"Where do you stay then?" Peyton asked.

"I's a servant for Miss Wimble. I do errands an' washin' an' things, an' she lets me stay in her barn at night. Even gives me a potato an' a carrot every day," she said with a smile that clearly affected Peyton.

Leinad saw the evidence of a broken heart in his father's eyes.

"Tess," Peyton said, "did you know that your smile is like bright sunshine on a cloudy day?"

Tess blushed through the dirt on her cheeks and looked shyly at the ground. Leinad figured this little girl rarely, if ever, received a compliment, and she apparently didn't know what to do with it.

"How would you like to take a ride in the country and have a hot meal?"

Tess looked back up at Peyton. "But mister, Miss Wimble won't take kindly ta me bein' late for chores. She says she owns me, an' that I'd better not run off or she'd come find me. I's already late now, an' I bet she's plenty mad."

As if on cue, a voice screeched from down the street. "Tess! You'd better git yourself home now!"

Leinad cringed at the sound of the woman's voice as she came closer.

"I got floors need sweepin' an' clothes need washin'. If you want your meal today, you'd better git after it!"

*Now we know where Tess learned her fine language skills,* Leinad thought.

The woman, her form plump and her countenance stern, ignored Peyton and Leinad as she marched up to Tess, grabbed her upper arm, and began to drag her down the street. Tess glanced over her shoulder at Peyton almost apologetically.

"Excuse me, madam." Peyton took a few strides to cover the distance between them.

The woman stopped and faced Peyton. "What do you want?"

"I don't believe the girl wants to go with you. Are you her mother?"

The woman squinted at Peyton. "I'm the only mother she's got, so she's mine."

"It sounds to me like you're more her master than her mother." Peyton's stern demeanor made it clear that he would not be dealt with lightly.

"So what if she's my servant. I've fed her for years, an' I figure that makes me her owner."

Peyton's anger was evident by his clenched jaw. "What do you figure she's worth to you?"

The woman's countenance changed to one of delight. "I figure I gotta have at least eighty shillings ta compensate for all the hassle she's caused me."

Peyton grabbed his money bag. "Here's five pounds— twenty shillings more than you asked." He placed the coins in the woman's hands and guided Tess away from her.

"I meant a hundred and eighty," the woman said, hoping to further her profit with protest.

"The deal is done!"

Peyton turned to face the woman squarely. She backed off immediately and walked up the street counting her treasure. She never turned to say good-bye to Tess.

Leinad looked at Tess and felt sympathy for her. He thought he saw dread in Tess's eyes, as though she feared her new owner could be worse than Miss Wimble.

Peyton waited until Miss Wimble was long gone; then he knelt on one knee and placed a gentle hand on Tess's shoulder. In this position, Tess was taller than Peyton, and he looked up into her eyes with compassion.

"Tess," he said softly, "the King never intended for people to be bought and sold like cattle. I did not buy you—I bought your freedom."

She looked into his eyes and, as she later told Leinad,

she felt real love for the first time in her life. Tears came to her eyes, and she hugged Peyton's neck. Peyton gently hugged her back, and his eyes brimmed with tears.

Leinad hoped that he would be as brave as his father—brave enough to reach through the dirt, the inconvenience, and the sacrifice to care for the unloved.

*Every person has a story,* he thought. *How many endure the same heartache and need the same compassion that Tess did?*

"Come on, Sunshine," Peyton said to Tess. "Let's take a ride to the country!"

## CHAPTER THREE

# A KINGDOM LOST

 Tess fell in love with country life immediately. The kindness Peyton and Leinad showed was so unknown to her that she could hardly accept it. Unfortunately, she knew nothing of personal hygiene, and Leinad enjoyed watching his father get flustered trying to explain the importance of basic personal cleanliness. It took four attempts at a bath before Tess emerged from the bathing room to Peyton's satisfaction. The brushes and combs that once stroked the hair of Leinad's mother now found use on soft strawberry-blond hair. Beneath the dirt and grime was the sparkling, freckled face of a pretty little girl.

Tess quickly fell into a routine of chores around the farm. Her years of serving Miss Wimble had developed an incredible efficiency in her work. She worked hard, long hours, and Leinad suspected she was trying to somehow repay the fatherly love and care that Peyton gave her. On many days, Peyton had to order her to stop her labor. The healthy meals she now ate strengthened her slender body and gave her energy to accompany her lively spirit.

Leinad assumed the role of big brother, though he was initially uncomfortable with it. Tess was succinct and Leinad liked that about her. He also enjoyed her infectious smile. Her manners and crude speech, however, left much to be desired. Leinad nearly winced every time she spoke.

"You two's goin' off ta practice again?" she asked as Leinad and Peyton donned their swords. She was sweeping the floor and asked the question without pausing her work.

"Yes, we are, Sunshine," Peyton said with a smile. The nickname he'd bestowed on her was a perfect fit. "Why don't you come with us and enjoy the fresh air today?"

"I's got too much work ta do, sir," Tess said, still not quite sure how to address Peyton. "Besides, I still ain't quite figured out what sword fightin's got ta do with farmin'." Tess's broom stopped, and she looked at Peyton with a genuine look of curiosity.

Peyton's smile broadened. "Okay, Tess, you can stay. But promise me you'll at least take a walk around the farm and enjoy a bit of the sunshine."

"Yes, sir." The broom's motion recommenced. "It's a fine time ta pick some blueberries anyways."

"Tess, you're not a slave anymore," Peyton said. "Besides, with you doing all the chores around here, you're going to end up making Leinad and me lazy!"

"I's jest doin' my part, Mr. Peyton, sir," Tess said sincerely. "Why, I's doin' less than I was and gettin' more than I had. I just want to make sure I's earnin' my keep."

Peyton walked toward Tess and stopped the broom.

"This is your home now, Tess. You do not have to earn a place here. It is yours forever if you want it." Leinad knew that his father was continually trying to reaffirm Tess and provide security for an insecure little girl.

THE SKY SEEMED BRIGHTER to Leinad today. As usual, training went well, and Leinad worked hard on developing patience and discipline. It was not natural for him though, and it was a difficult lesson to learn.

"How are you doing with a young lady in the house, Leinad?" Peyton asked as he and Leinad walked toward their favorite oak tree for a time of rest.

Leinad smiled at the thought of Tess. "I'm doing okay, although I have to admit it's taking some adjustment."

"Yes, I agree," said Peyton. "I know that bringing her into our home is a disruption, but something about that little girl just grabbed my heart, and I couldn't turn my back on her that day in town."

"She sure has a way of telling it like it is, doesn't she, Father?" Leinad said, preparing his father for a subject that was nagging his mind.

"Yes, she's a pretty discerning little lass."

Leinad was silent for a moment. "Father, Tess is right about farming and sword fighting, and I feel less and less like a farmer with every passing day."

Peyton responded to Leinad's comment with a moment of silence, then put his arm around his son's shoulder as they neared the oak.

"Leinad, your insight is true. Farming is honorable, but

I have prepared you for a much greater calling."

The two found rest as they sat against the oak and drank cool water from their flasks.

"Son, you are a boy on the verge of manhood. I sense that you are looking for more purpose in this life than to eat and sleep and wait for the next day's sunrise. Am I right?"

"Yes, Father. I'm just not sure what that purpose is or how to find it."

"What you are feeling is the pull on your heart to fulfill a greater calling…a calling for which I am preparing you."

Leinad was both curious and confused.

"Which of my teachings are most important to you, Leinad?" Peyton asked.

Leinad reflected on the years of training and teaching his father had given him. Only now was he beginning to realize that nothing his father did or taught was by accident. All was done with purpose. He thought about the intense sword training. Although he felt confident with the sword, there was no one to compare his skills to other than his father, and he believed he was far below that level of mastery. He thought about the academic teachings of quill and ink and speech. He thought of the daily reinforcement of character building that his father carefully grafted into his spirit. All of this, and yet he knew what was worth much more.

"To be loyal to the King, even unto death, and to have compassion for my fellow man," Leinad said with conviction.

"And why is this so important, son?"

"Because the King is good and worthy of our loyalty," Leinad said.

"But you have not even met the King."

Leinad leaned forward from the tree and turned to question his father's eyes. This was new ground, and he approached curiously and cautiously. Something in his soul was yearning for more.

"No, I have not met the King...but you have. I have learned from you, I have questioned you, but most of all I have watched you. I know you, Father. There is not another man in the kingdom more honest, generous, compassionate, or courageous than you. If the King deserves the complete loyalty you give Him, then I do not need to see Him face-to-face to know that He is worthy of my complete loyalty as well."

Peyton lowered his eyes. Leinad sensed a sadness overcome his father and did not understand why. An awkward silence ensued, broken only by the voice of a meadow bird. It was Peyton who spoke first.

"I am thankful you see the King for who He really is and that your loyalty is sure, but I am not worthy of the high praise you give me." Peyton turned slightly from his son and seemed to struggle to maintain a steady voice.

"Before you were born, I once failed the King."

Leinad could not make himself see his father as anything other than what he was now, and there was no flaw in his character. Besides, how could a common farmer fail the King in any significant way? Never before had his father been so vulnerable with him. Leinad was not sure how to proceed.

"Father, you are a man of unfailing loyalty to the King. Any offense or neglect that you might have committed has surely been forgiven."

"Yes." Peyton took a deep breath. "But my failure will haunt me to my death."

Peyton turned back to face his son and placed a firm grip on his shoulder. "The King's heart is deep for the people of this land, and though you have not met Him, He knows you."

"Father, where is the King, and why hasn't He established His kingdom in Arrethtrae?" Leinad asked.

"The King lives in His kingdom across the Great Sea. From all I have heard, it is a kingdom like no other. It is a kingdom of wealth, beauty, and mysterious wonders. It has even been said that there is a spice there that brings healing to the body...even the restoring of youth to the old.

"Some time ago, there was a rebellion in this glorious kingdom, led by none other than the King's first warrior, Lucius. Lucius was a brilliant swordsman and tactician. He was able to entice one-third of the King's best warriors to join him in his attempt to overthrow the King. However, his attempt was thwarted, and instead he and his rebellious warriors fled across the sea to come to Arrethtrae, our land. You see, Leinad, Lucius was so full of pride and jealousy that when he lost the war, he wanted to take revenge on the King. He knew that the King loved this beautiful land and the people in it and that He had planted a new kingdom here. Lucius came here to destroy the land and to destroy the people."

Leinad knew somehow that his father's words were connected to the higher calling they had talked about earlier...a calling to which Leinad was only now opening his heart.

"I have protected you from much of the anguish this kingdom has endured as a result of Lucius's influence. But one day you must face those hardships, for the paradise of the original kingdom is lost." Peyton paused, and Leinad was compelled to focus on every word his father spoke.

"Leinad, what I am going to tell you is hard for me, but it is necessary for you to understand who you are and how this all applies to you," Peyton said as Leinad swallowed the last bite of some fruit and tossed the remains.

Leinad adjusted himself so he could face his father and waited patiently for him to gather his words.

"Many years before you were born, the King found a promising young man and woman to help Him begin a new kingdom. It was to be a kingdom of peace, harmony, and prosperity…a kingdom of promise and hope." Peyton paused and took a deep breath. "Your mother and I were that man and woman, Leinad, and we were chosen to usher in the beginning of this paradise."

Leinad replayed the words in his mind to make sure he had not misheard. Were they not spoken by his father, he would have thought them to be the boastings of an idiot.

"Bear with me, son, and all will make sense when you've heard it in its entirety. Why the King chose me I will never know, for I was certainly undeserving. That is what I find so remarkable about the King—He chooses the lowly to accomplish the lofty. The beautiful land of Arrethtrae has always been in the center of the King's heart. It was a glorious time—the dawn of a kingdom, and your mother and I were a central part of it. The King built a majestic castle—no, it was a palace. The great hall in the keep was grand indeed. The entire palace was ornate, with rare and exquisite tapestries and decorations. It was built from the finest timbers and stone of the land. There were many magnificent courtyards, but your mother's favorite place to be was in the beautiful, lush garden. She loved to walk beneath the shade of the trees and smell the fragrant flowers.

Leinad saw the ache in Peyton's heart through his eyes as he reminisced about his time with his wife.

"We were young, in love, and living a life that no one could ever believe. The King appointed servants, huntsmen, cooks, and a garrison of guards to serve and protect the palace. We were the lord and lady of the land. I came to know the King personally, Leinad!"

"Father, how can this be?" Leinad said. "Friends with the King? All I know is this life of farming, and I have known nothing else. How can this be?"

"Perhaps I have kept this from you for too long, but you have never known me to exaggerate. Nevertheless, what I tell you is true. The King befriended me. He trained me in the art of the sword by day and walked with me in the cool of the garden by evening. I will serve no other, for there is no other like Him. I came to know the purity and goodness of His heart, the power and strength of His arm, and the wisdom and mercy of His judgment. Many men have tried to rule as king and many more are to come, but only He is worthy and deserving.

"The King wanted me to rule by proxy, for He spent most of His time across the sea. In His absence, I was to govern the land. He trusted me with a fresh, new kingdom."

Peyton's eyes saddened, and the pain in his voice was obvious.

"Father, no matter the tale, I will not judge you." Leinad rested a hand on his father's arm and looked earnestly into his eyes. "What I hear will not change what I know to be a man of honor. Please let me learn that I might not fail. There is a fire that kindles in my heart, and I don't know why or understand it. Somehow I know it is connected to you, the King, and your story."

"Late one summer day," Peyton continued, "a tall, handsome man came to the gate of our palace bearing gifts he claimed to be both rare and exquisite. Except for his footman and driver, this noble-looking gentleman was alone, and your mother and I allowed him and his carriage entry through the gate and into the courtyard. He introduced himself as Lord Sinjon, from the distant land of Hadenborough. He did indeed carry fine linen, spices, and other gifts that we had never seen before. Your mother was taken with the quality of the items.

"But the King had warned us not to receive gifts of any kind from those we did not know. 'Surely, madam,' the gentleman said to your mother, 'the King did not intend for you to refuse such beautiful gifts as these from a man of my stature, did He? After all, what harm can come from accepting one small gift of adoration?' I watched her struggle with principles and loyalty in silence. Finally she yielded to his insistence, for these were gifts that no one in the kingdom had acquired. I watched her delicate hand reach forth and receive the gifts, and I said nothing…nothing, Leinad! That was my crime, which I shall live with forever."

Peyton paused, closed his eyes, and lowered his head. For the first time in his life, Leinad saw his father as a fellow flawed human being instead of the infallible man that he had unfairly esteemed him to be. Leinad let his father recover himself in silence.

"Having received the gifts, we felt obligated to offer food and rest to Lord Sinjon and his servants, for evening was upon us," Peyton continued. "The man was extremely polite and considerate, a gentleman in every way. He had dark hair and sharp features. His conversation was smooth and intriguing. Despite all this, I felt a slight foreboding about him. Before turning in for the night, I posted guards near the guest quarters as a precaution. What I did not know was that across the sea, a rebellion had taken place and Arrethtrae would quickly be swept up in the destructive storm of its vengeance.

"In the middle of the night, I was awakened by the sound of your mother pleading for help. I opened my eyes to a nightmare of horror. At the foot of my bed stood Lord Sinjon with a knife across your mother's throat. I leaped from my bed, but he pressed the knife tighter against her throat. 'Don't be stupid!' he said. His voice and countenance were so loathsome that I could hardly believe it was the same man we had entertained a few hours earlier. I called for the guards, but Sinjon laughed a vile laugh. 'We treated you as a guest, and you lied to us,' I said. He smiled condescendingly. 'Yes,' he said, 'it is what I do best. Out!' He motioned toward the door of our bedchamber. The fear in your mother's eyes matched the fear in my heart. I walked ahead of them to the door and passed into the great hall. Many of my guards lay dead, and I heard the occasional clash of swords in the distance. Within the great hall stood twenty to thirty of the largest, fiercest looking warriors I have ever seen. Evidently the footman and driver were also two of his warriors, and they had quietly overtaken the gate guards to allow Sinjon's evil force entrance to the palace.

"A nightmarish tragedy was unfolding before my eyes as the reality of my foolish disobedience pierced my heart. My men were dead and my wife was held in the grip of a murderous liar. 'Sinjon, though you kill us all, the King will return and retake this palace from you!' I said with as much force as I could muster. He glared at me. 'I do not want this palace, fool,' he said with hatred and spite in his eyes. 'I want the entire kingdom! I will soon be king of all of Arrethtrae!' He smiled in his arrogance as his warriors in the hall saluted him with their swords.

"We were forced into the main courtyard, where more death and destruction awaited. I knew that the chilled black night revealed only a small portion of the devastation Sinjon had wreaked on the palace. His warriors were massive and ruthless. There were hundreds of his men, and they had completely taken the palace. Once they had come inside the outer wall, my garrison didn't have a chance, and it was I who had let them enter. I wanted to return to the dust from which I came and erase my existence, but my heart kept beating.

"He turned us around to see the great palace. 'Burn everything that will burn, and destroy everything else,' he ordered his men. Within a few moments, unquenchable flames illuminated the night, revealing the totality of Sinjon's assault. 'Kneel!' he said, and one of his men forced me to my knees before him. He threw your mother to the ground beside me. She was a strong woman, your mother, but I saw the reflection of the glowing flames in the tears on her cheeks as we witnessed the end of our paradise. I put my arm around her for what I believed to be our final embrace.

"Sinjon stood before us, reveling in his power over us—in the King's destroyed future for Arrethtrae. One of his warriors approached from the great hall. 'My Lord, it is done!' he said. 'Excellent!' Sinjon exclaimed. 'Gather the men outside the gate, and wait for me while I deal with these two.' 'Who are you?' I asked as his men retreated from their brutal handiwork toward the main gate. Sinjon looked down on us through narrowed eyes with his chin raised and a sword drawn. He paused. 'I *was* the King's principal warrior, second only to the Prince. Now I *am* the King's principal enemy, second to no one! I am Lucius!'"

"Lucius?" Leinad said.

"Yes, the Dark Knight!"

"He is real, then? Not just a mythical evil warrior?" Leinad asked.

"He is very real, unfortunately. And having witnessed the heinous actions he and his men were capable of, I knew that our death was imminent. 'Please spare the life of my wife. There is no need for her death,' I pleaded with him. He slowly and silently walked behind us, and I covered your mother's back with my body, fully expecting his blade to slice through me at any moment. As he returned to the front, he placed the tip of his blade beneath my chin, forcing me to look up at him as he spoke. 'Your fate will be worse than a quick death, peasant. You must now face your pathetic King and explain how you destroyed His plan for the kingdom. I want the King to see how His miserable nobles completely failed Him. No, I will not be so merciful as to kill you now. You have done that to the kingdom and to your own future. That is satisfaction—true satisfaction for me.'"

Peyton paused and stared at nothing.

"What happened next, Father?" Leinad prompted tenderly.

"Lucius and his warriors left the palace and disappeared into the night. And then we did a cowardly thing, Leinad. We were so ashamed and afraid that we fled into the hills and found a cave to hide ourselves in. The King was returning soon, and we could not bear to face Him." Peyton covered his face with his hands and rubbed his eyes.

Leinad could feel the pain of his father. Part of him wished he had not heard this story, for he was not comfortable with his father being so vulnerable with him. But deep within him there was an intense desire to know it all. So he waited for his father to continue.

Peyton lowered his hands and covered his pursed lips. Though his eyes were red and his voice quavered, he resumed the story for his son.

"The King searched for us. I heard Him call, but we were afraid and ashamed. I had cost Him too much. I'd hoped He would think we were dead and forget about us, but somehow He knew we were alive, and so He searched. Finally I could stand it no longer, and I called to Him from our cave.

As He approached, He ordered His warriors to stay behind. We knelt with our faces to the ground. Facing the shame of our King was worse than facing the sword of Lucius. He dismounted from His steed and stood before us. The moment of silence that followed as I felt His gaze on my neck was unbearable. Softly He spoke, 'Peyton…Dinan.' I could not restrain my tears of sorrow and repentance. 'My King,' I said and slowly lifted my eyes to see the disappointment in His majestic face. 'We…I have failed You. I have destroyed Your palace…Your future kingdom. Take my life, my Lord, for I am not worthy to live.' The quiet tears of your mother joined mine.

"'Rise,' said the King. 'The cost of your failure is great…but I forgive you. You must understand that I am a merciful king, but I am also a just king. Through your weakness, Lucius has destroyed the future of many people. You and Dinan must leave this region and establish a farm in the Plains of Kerr. My plans for Arrethtrae will follow a different course now. Raise your children to honor Me, and through them I will bring victory over Lucius and peace to the land of Arrethtrae.'"

Peyton turned to his son and placed a hand on his shoulder. "Leinad," he said quietly, "that is how I have raised you…to honor the King. Where I have failed, you must not. Somehow the King will use you to help establish His kingdom here in Arrethtrae."

"But Father, why doesn't the King bring His warriors to Arrethtrae, conquer Lucius, and establish His kingdom? I am just a boy…I could never hope to accomplish what you could not."

"The King does not want devotion through force, Leinad. He wants a kingdom of people who love Him because they want to love Him, not because they are forced to. He loves the land, and He loves these people. He has chosen a different way...a more excellent way. This is why you are feeling less and less like a farmer every day. Stay strong—stay true—stay loyal!"

"I will, Father. I swear it," Leinad said. "But what am I supposed to do?"

Leinad felt his father's eyes penetrate his soul.

"I wish I could answer that for you, son, but I truly don't know. That is a question for which you alone must discover the answer."

Leinad's small world was now much bigger. In just a few moments, the solid ground of his life had shifted beneath him. His father...his farm...his life was not what it appeared to be. Was anything he believed in still anchored and unchanged? He asked himself and searched. He found one unmovable truth...the King was!

# YESTERDAY'S END

Leinad loved to hunt game. His accuracy with a bow and arrow was uncanny. Successful hunting required patience, something Leinad usually found difficult to practice. However, the quiet realm of the forest afforded Leinad an opportunity to think and reflect, which he found himself doing quite frequently lately.

Today Peyton had encouraged Leinad to hunt alone, saying he needed to accomplish some things around the farm. "Besides," Peyton had said, "I think you could probably use some time to yourself."

Leinad always hunted on foot in the forest. Horses were noisy, and he preferred to blend with his surroundings as much as possible. He was disappointed and somewhat surprised at the lack of game. It was already midmorning and he was still empty-handed. The overcast skies made the forest walls feel closer than usual, and Leinad felt an uneasiness that would not dissipate no matter how hard he tried. The deeper he journeyed into the forest, the deeper his apprehension became.

*What is wrong with me?* Leinad thought. *I feel like jumping out of my skin and for no reason.*

Leinad suddenly became aware of the silence of the forest. It was an abnormal silence. There were no birds singing, squirrels chirping, or even wind rustling the leaves of the trees. A deadly still engulfed him. Something was wrong! Though he had entered this forest a thousand times, it was a different forest today.

Leinad became as silent and as still as the forest. All of his senses were alert and craved a response, but there was none. His apprehension slowly transformed into the ugly beast of fear—small at first but growing. He could not deny that he now felt as though he was no longer the hunter, but the hunted. And the predator was unknown. He had seen this arena before, only this time *he* was the deer that felt danger in every fiber of his body. The only comfort Leinad could find was in the fact that he was no longer making noise, hoping that his presence would be lost in the silence of a forest that seemed much darker now than just moments ago. Unfortunately, he knew that even this small remaining comfort must end. Reason told him it was folly to wait for an unknown outcome he had no control over. He must gain control of his fear and either retreat or discover his predator before his predator discovered him.

He wanted to run but did not dare. Instead, he forced himself to take his first step out of fear and silence—one step deeper into the forest. He froze again and listened. The beating of his heart and his breathing seemed too loud to hear above. One more step—listen. Another— listen. His small advances fueled his resolve to turn back the encroaching panic. He continued cautiously, moving toward an unknown enemy and an unknown fate.

The distant neigh of a horse pounded through the silence and dropped Leinad instantly to the ground. It was all he heard, but it was enough to tell him that he was probably still undetected. It also gave him a direction to travel, and he moved stealthily and slightly faster now. Though the forest hid its origin, Leinad now heard the distinct sounds of a breaking encampment. He knelt near a large tree and strained to filter voices from the rest. There were many men…and many weapons.

Leinad knew he must get closer if he was going to hear any conversation. He left his crouched position, stepped around the tree, and came face-to-face with all the fear he was fighting to conquer. A massive hand encircled Leinad's throat. He dropped his bow and instinctively clutched the hand that threatened his life as it pulled him toward the face of a huge man.

"I see we have a little rat spying upon us," a gruff voice snarled.

Leinad stood on his toes to relieve some of the pain in his neck.

"I should very much like to kill you here, but the commander will want to see you first, rat."

The man released Leinad and pushed him with the tip of his sword toward the sounds of the encampment. Leinad felt the warm tickle of his own blood trickle down his back.

Soon Leinad found himself in the midst of a dark and

ominous contingent of warriors. All were large. All were well fitted for war. The sword in his back pushed him toward a circle of men in the center of the encampment.

"Where are your men now?" came the voice of one of the men.

Leinad could see that the man's posture and commanding presence evoked a fearful respect from the rest of the men.

"On the western edge of the forest," came the reply from one of the men on the opposite side of the circle. The man bore a grotesque scar on his forehead. "We can be ready to ride by midday." Though sinister looking, the scarred man was not an equal with the commander or any of the other men for that matter. Their attitude toward him was one of tolerance.

"Midday may be too late," the commander said sharply. "I suggest you motivate them to move faster, or you may not have any men to command!"

"Commander," spoke the owner of the sword in Leinad's back, "forgive the intrusion, but I found this rat snooping about the camp."

He forced Leinad into the circle to face the commander.

Leinad instantly became the spectacle of the six men. The steel glares made him feel as though he was being prepared for execution. It was clear to him that the intentions of these men were comprised of dark deeds. The fear he had momentarily conquered earlier in the forest rushed back upon him.

The commander stepped toward Leinad and glared at him with intense disdain. He was a tall, handsome man with sharp features and dark eyes. Leinad lowered his eyes in fearful submission, unable to bear the hatred that emanated from the commander's fierce countenance.

"What did you hear, boy?" the commander asked.

Leinad's only reply was silence. He knew his fate was sealed regardless of what he said. His silence also protected the small shred of pride he had left by not revealing the fear in his heart through a voice that was sure to tremble.

A warrior approached on horseback and broke the silence. "All of the men are mounted and ready, Commander."

The commander relinquished his glare on Leinad and walked toward his waiting steed. As he mounted, so did the rest of the men, with the exception of the scarred man behind Leinad.

"Kill him and dispose of him as you see fit, Zane," the commander said to the scarred man. As he positioned his steed and motioned to his men, he turned again toward the man called Zane and smiled an evil smile. "I have some unfinished business to attend to."

He kicked his horse and led his entourage of dark warriors into the forest…in the direction Leinad had come from.

The quiet of the forest soon returned as the band of warriors disappeared into its depths. Leinad turned his head slightly to verify the presence of the scarred man. As he did, he heard and saw the man draw his sword from his scabbard. Leinad was ashamed to think it, but all the good he had lived seemed irrelevant at the moment, and he thought how much better it would be if he had not been born.

He heard the man take two steps toward his back and

readied himself to flee or fight; he couldn't decide. *If only I had my sword, at least I would have a chance*, he thought.

"This was a bad day for you to wander into the forest, boy," the man said as he slowly circled around to the front of Leinad. "You see, I have some pressing business to attend to, and I haven't time to waste." He held the sword before him, close to Leinad's throat. As the man looked full into Leinad's face for the first time, Leinad saw a glimmer of uncertainty in his eyes.

He could not help gazing at the scar that crossed the man's forehead. He felt an uneasy familiarity about the man even though he had never seen him before.

The man squinted at Leinad and lowered his sword. "Where do you live, boy?"

Leinad did not dare answer for fear of bringing danger to his father and Tess. His silence might bring his death more quickly, but he knew there was no other choice to make.

The man raised his sword in anger. "I can kill you in an instant, boy. Now where do you live?"

"You will kill me anyway, and my words of betrayal to my family will haunt me beyond the doors of death," Leinad said.

Surprisingly, the man's anger was somewhat abated by Leinad's answer, and he once again lowered his sword.

"Remove your shoes," he said.

Leinad crouched down and complied with the man's order.

"Now that you cannot flee so easily, I will give you an opportunity to provide some sport for me. It is much more enjoyable to kill in a fight than to kill the defenseless." He walked a few paces to his horse, withdrew a second sword, and threw it toward Leinad's bare feet.

"Do your best, boy. I am in a hurry, but I haven't felt the thrill of a fight for some time."

Leinad stared at the man in disbelief and then at the sword at his feet.

"Pick it up, boy! Hold it in front of you. I haven't much time to waste."

Leinad bent down to retrieve the sword, but he kept his eye on the man. As he lifted the sword in front of him, the scarred man yelled and threw one swift cut at Leinad, who instinctively blocked the cut and fell back into a defensive posture. The man cocked his head to one side as he stared at Leinad.

"You did not startle as I would expect. Let us see if you are truly brave or just numb with fear."

Leinad felt the blood coursing through his muscles as his mind awakened his body's purpose from that of captive to that of sword fighter. His grip became firm and his eyes narrowed. The scarred man watched the transformation, and it was apparent that he was now aware of his mistake. He faced a formidable challenge.

The man advanced on Leinad with a quick combination of cuts and slices. Leinad met each attack with the precision of an experienced sword fighter. His mind automatically controlled his muscles to meet each volley of attacks while simultaneously analyzing the strengths and weaknesses of the man. Unable to penetrate Leinad's defenses, the man's fervent attacks were a clear indication that he was trying to quell his mounting apprehension.

Leinad blocked a head-high cut with the flat of his blade and thwarted a conservative thrust off to his left. Then he attacked with a cut combination from the left and above. The man narrowly escaped the deadly edge of Leinad's sword and began falling back for the first time since the fight began.

Leinad maintained the offensive and methodically advanced on the man. His blade raced toward the man's torso but met steel instead of flesh. He quickly added a vertical cut, but it too was thwarted. His opponent was no amateur, and it was clear that Leinad would have to be at his best in order to survive this encounter.

In response to Leinad's offensive moves, the man became deathly aggressive and countered with an onslaught of cuts and slices. Leinad once again found himself retreating while deflecting each powerful blow. The two swords clashed with great speed time after time to fill the forest stage with an unusual melodic beat. In his retreat, Leinad saw in his peripheral vision a large tree off to his right, and he was thankful that he had not backed into it or stumbled on its exposed roots.

Just then the scarred man brought a powerful slice from Leinad's left, aimed at his torso. Rather than meet the blow, Leinad fell to the forest floor and allowed the slice to pass above his head. The man's sword became embedded in the trunk of the tree as Leinad had hoped. Knowing the man was unable to instantly recover, Leinad chanced an upward thrust from his kneeling position, and the man dodged quickly to his left.

He was too late. His leather tunic deflected Leinad's blade slightly, but not enough to prevent it from slicing the tender skin on his right side. The wound was agonizingly painful, as evidenced by the man's scream, but probably not fatal. Leinad tried to recover from the thrust, but the man drove his knee into Leinad's head, which sent him reeling to the ground.

The blow nearly knocked Leinad unconscious. He desperately fought to regain his senses and rise to his feet. Dizzy and unfocused, he wondered when he too would feel the deadly steel of a blade penetrate his body. He stumbled away from where he knew the man had last been. Leinad grabbed his head with his hands to help steady himself, and his vision cleared slightly. He looked toward the tree, nearly ten paces away, and saw the man clutching his side in a kneeling position. Leinad realized that his sword must have cut deeper than he thought.

It was only then that he realized he was without his sword. The blow to his head had caused him to release his grip. His sword lay near the man, and Leinad did not dare retrieve it. His only chance now was to flee.

He heard the man gasp, "Run, boy! My revenge will be in your death tomorrow!" The man coughed and moaned as he fell further to the ground.

Leinad backed away from the scarred man. He had never injured, let alone killed, anyone before. The distant sound of approaching horses forced him to retreat quickly. He turned and began to run across the forest floor as fast as his bare feet would take him. He regretted not retrieving his shoes before launching his escape, but now it was too late. He chose a direction slightly off what would be toward home.

Fully expecting to hear the hooves of chasing horses, Leinad tried to place as much distance between himself and them as possible. *Now I really am the hunted,* he thought. Seconds turned to minutes, and his feet began to bleed. He ran until he felt as though his lungs would burst. Finally he collapsed behind the shelter of a fallen tree to regain some air and spot his would-be hunters. But there was no pursuit.

Leinad's mind raced through the questions that filled it. *Who were these men? Where did they come from? What was their mission?* The sickening feeling in the pit of his stomach was no longer caused by his flight, but by what he might discover ahead of him. Having verified that he was not being pursued, he resumed his run at a pace he could maintain and altered his direction toward home. As he ran, his anxiety grew. Regardless of the final destination of the band of warriors that earlier had headed south, their direction would take them straight to his father's farm. The mere thought made him quicken his pace.

Leinad finally cleared the forest edge and began the trek across the grassy fields and hills. He tried to ignore the blood that oozed from his swollen feet. The fresh imprints in the soil of many horses made him painfully aware that others had taken this same path earlier.

Leinad dropped to the ground just prior to the final ridge that blocked the view of his farm. He closed his eyes and hoped against hope that he would once again see the serene and peaceful farmyard waiting for him. He slowly crawled to the crest of the ridge and looked toward home.

The horror Leinad had dreaded quickly became reality. The entire contingent of vicious warriors occupied the farmyard. His father was held in the grip of two massive warriors, and the commander was facing him with his sword drawn. Leinad searched for Tess, but he could not see her. He was too far away to hear distinct words but close enough to hear their voices.

Leinad reasoned that there must be some connection between his father's previous life and this man who commanded these dark warriors. If that was so, he knew that his father's life was in serious jeopardy. Leinad felt completely helpless, and yet he knew he must do something. As he desperately tried to think of a course of action, he witnessed the unthinkable. The commander plunged his sword into Peyton's torso.

It was too much for Leinad to bear in silence. He started to rise up and scream, but a large hand covered his mouth as a heavily muscled arm pressed him facedown to the ground. Only a muffled scream of anger and fear escaped through the powerful fingers that entrapped his lips. Leinad struggled, but the weight of another body pressed him hard to the ground.

A deep whisper entered his ear. "You will only be killed as well!"

Leinad recognized the accent that belonged to only one man—Gabrik—and quit his struggle.

Gabrik slowly released his grip on Leinad and turned him over on his back.

"You must stay in control, Leinad," Gabrik said sternly. "Your father would expect nothing less."

"We must do something!" Leinad said as he fought back rage and tears.

"Even if I had a dozen of my best men, it would be suicide to take on Lucius under these conditions!" Gabrik said with as much pain in his voice as Leinad felt in his own heart.

"The Dark Knight?" Leinad whispered. The mere sound of those words passing his lips struck fear in his bosom. He had been face-to-face with the archenemy of the King, and he hadn't even known it.

Gabrik crawled slowly to the ridge on his elbows and knees to reconnoiter the situation. Leinad remained motionless on his back and tried to make sense of these bizarre events.

After a time, Gabrik retreated to Leinad's position and placed a clenched fist to his lips, momentarily lost in deep thought.

Leinad suddenly became aware that Gabrik was much more than a town blacksmith. He rose to a low sitting position and stared at Gabrik. Knowing that his father was dead or dying and that he could do nothing was agonizing.

"Gabrik," he said softly. "What do we do?"

"We have no choice but to remain unseen until they leave," Gabrik said.

"When I left the farm this morning, there was a little girl with my father, and I haven't seen her yet. Have you?"

Gabrik turned and looked at Leinad. "No, I have not. We must hope she is hidden away someplace."

"We have a cellar beneath the kitchen floorboards. Maybe my father had enough time to hide her there."

"Maybe," Gabrik said softly. "Maybe."

Leinad closed his eyes, but the image of his father being

pierced was vividly imprinted on his mind. He turned away from Gabrik to hide the tears forming in his eyes.

Gabrik returned to his lookout position at the top of the ridge. "Leinad! They are leaving," he whispered and motioned for him to join him.

Leinad peered over the ridge and into the horror that would change his life forever.

He saw his father lying motionless on the ground. Lucius mounted and gave an order to his men. Torches were set aflame and thrown onto the house. Lucius reared his horse and led his men off the farm to the northeast.

Once Lucius and his men were beyond sight, Gabrik and Leinad ran to Peyton. Leinad felt as though he were running in place, for each moment that passed was a moment too long.

"Father!" he cried as he fell to Peyton's side.

Peyton was still breathing, but his breaths were short and raspy. He opened his eyes. The pained look on his face was nearly unbearable for Leinad. Gabrik had already torn open Peyton's tunic and was trying to stop the blood loss.

"Leinad…" Peyton gasped. "Tess…cellar!"

Leinad looked at the burning house, which would soon be engulfed in flames. He did not want to leave his father, but he knew that he must.

"Leinad," Gabrik said, "I must help your father, for every moment counts. Go find the girl!"

Leinad ran into the smoke-filled house and was forced to the floor by the noxious fumes. There he found some breathable air and crawled into the kitchen. He found the cellar floorboards and removed them as quickly as possible.

"Tess!" Leinad screamed through the smoke and fire.

The temperature was rising quickly, and he was worried that the roof might collapse at any moment.

"Here I am, Leinad! Here!" Tess screamed.

She climbed the ladder up to the kitchen floor, and Leinad pulled her out. Tess stood to run, but Leinad pulled her down beside him.

"Crawl to the door!" he said and pointed in that direction.

Leinad followed close behind her, and they made their way out of the burning house. They both fell to the ground and gasped for air. Leinad forced himself to his feet and ran back to his father's side. He looked at Gabrik for some sign of hope, but Gabrik refused to pause in his desperate work to save Peyton's life. He applied a sweet-smelling salve to the wound and pressed a clean cloth against the river of blood.

Peyton grabbed Leinad's arm weakly. "Tess?" he whispered to Leinad.

"She is safe," Leinad said.

Peyton closed his eyes for a brief moment of relief.

"Father, hang on! You cannot die!"

Peyton opened his eyes and looked lovingly at his son. "Leinad…I…love you." Peyton coughed and his lips turned red from the bleeding within his body. "I have prepared you for a greater purpose…stay true to the King." Peyton struggled for breath. "Discover the promise and…beware…of…your brother!"

Peyton's grasp on Leinad's arm loosened, and his arm fell to the ground. The last bit of air escaped from his lungs, and he died.

"No!" Leinad cradled his father close to his breast. Peyton's final words were temporarily lost in an avalanche of emotion. A flood of tears ran down his cheeks and onto the pale face of his father. His moans of mourning were hidden beneath the crash of the farmhouse and the raging fire that engulfed the remaining timber.

"I'm sorry, Leinad," Gabrik said. "The wound was too severe. I did everything I could."

Tess made her way to Peyton's body and knelt across from Leinad. Though she was well acquainted with hardship, Peyton's death crushed her softening heart. She cried the tears of a lost child. Leinad's tears of sorrow could not quench his burning anger.


GABRIK HELPED LEINAD bury Peyton next to his beloved wife, Dinan, on the lush hillside that welcomed the sun each morning near the farmhouse. The somber trio gave honor to Peyton and Dinan in reverent silence. Never before had Leinad felt so alone.

Leinad knelt down and grabbed a handful of the cool, soft dirt. Digging the grave had given some respite to the intense sorrow Leinad felt, but in the stillness of the moment, grief once again pressed hard upon his soul, and he could not restrain his tears. He wept bitterly for his father.

He had felt the same deep hurt in his heart eight years ago when he and his father stood over his mother's grave. This time there was no one to comfort him as his father had…no one to hug him and give him the courage to carry on. His sorrow penetrated to his bones.

Leinad fought through the intense feelings of anger and revenge to search for some purpose that would persuade him to press forward. After a few moments, Tess placed a gentle hand on his shoulder. He looked up at her and then at Gabrik with moistened eyes.

"Why, Gabrik? Why?"

The impact of an ancient war cut deep into Leinad's heart, and he knew that Gabrik felt it too.

"Because Lucius knew that your father was the key to the kingdom."

"So now that he is dead, hope is dead. And what have we gained?" Leinad asked bitterly.

"No, Leinad," Gabrik said. "The hope lives on!"

## CHAPTER FIVE

# A SWORD AND A MISSION

 Leinad stood motionless at his father's grave long after the shadows had reversed their direction. He clung in desperation to the memories of his father, afraid that they too might fade like those of his mother. Though in his mind he knew that his father was gone, it did not feel real. The distance of time had not yet seared that truth into his heart.

As he raced through the memories of his father, he could not stop before he rushed once again into the tragedies that had occurred earlier that day. It was only then that Leinad remembered in astonishment the words his father had spoken just prior to his death. The words sounded in his mind almost as though his father were still speaking them. *I love you…I have prepared you for a greater purpose…stay true to the King…discover the promise and…beware…of…your brother!*

Broken from his trance, Leinad ran back to the ruins of the farmhouse. Tess was searching through the blackened remains and had found the scorched combs Peyton had given her. Though unusable, she held them as though they were a treasure to her.

"Tess!" he exclaimed, worried that the only one who might be able to answer his questions was gone. "Where is Gabrik?"

"I don't know, Leinad," she said, somewhat amazed at Leinad's sudden enthusiasm.

"Gabrik!" Leinad called, searching the surrounding country.

Gabrik peaked a nearby rise in the terrain and cantered his horse toward the farmyard. Just then, along the same ridgeline but a good distance to the north, another rider appeared. His horse reared and neighed. Gabrik stopped his horse and turned to look at the rider, as did Leinad and Tess. The rider was in full battle dress, covered in armor from his neck to his feet. His presence was threatening.

Leinad felt apprehensive, and his mind struggled with many questions. Was this a scout for an entire army or a lone rider? Was he hostile or friendly? With no sword or horse, Leinad could not fight or flee. How could he protect Tess if he needed to?

The rider raised both of his arms into the air, then lowered them below his waist and bowed his head. Leinad saw Gabrik reply to the rider with the same gesture. Then Gabrik and the rider rode toward each other. Their exchange diffused the tension, and Leinad relaxed somewhat.

"What is it, Leinad?" Tess asked.

Leinad turned to see her sweet face covered with streaks of

soot, and he was reminded of the day he saw her on the streets in Mankin. It was the first time he'd had thoughts of someone other than himself since the tragedy of the morning. He was ashamed that he thought he was the only one truly hurting.

"I'm not sure, Sunshine," Leinad said.

Tess smiled slightly. He addressed her with the nickname Peyton had given her. It seemed to bring her comfort, and Leinad felt it too.

"Thanks fer savin' me from the fire, Leinad." Tess wrapped her arms around his waist and squeezed him.

Unsure of what to do, he gave her a quick hug back.

"It was, uh, nothing, but you're welcome," Leinad said. Tess let loose and gave Leinad some room.

"What we gonna do now?" she asked.

Leinad watched intently as Gabrik and the rider covered the remaining distance between them.

"I don't know," Leinad said, still focused on the distant figures. "I just don't know. I know how to farm, and we've still got the land. I guess we'll continue on."

Leinad suddenly became aware that he alone was responsible for Tess now. The burden of providing for, teaching, nurturing, and protecting another seemed so easy for his father, but the thought of it nearly panicked Leinad.

Leinad saw Gabrik and the rider salute each other and separate. The rider turned back north from where he came, and Gabrik directed his horse toward Leinad and Tess at a pace significantly faster than earlier. When he drew near, he slowed his horse to a halt and dismounted.

Leinad approached him and looked up into Gabrik's eyes—eyes he once feared, but that was no longer true. His quest for answers overpowered any inhibition he might have once felt.

"You heard my father's last words, and I think you know what they mean. Who are you, Gabrik?" The question was simple. Leinad knew that its answer would go far beyond that of "the blacksmith of Mankin."

Gabrik looked at Leinad, then turned to adjust some leather straps on his horse. There was an urgency in his movements that hadn't been there earlier. The muscles rippled across his back.

"I am a servant…a servant of the King. I am a messenger. I am a guardian." He turned his head toward Leinad. "I am a Silent Warrior." He finished his adjustments and turned squarely to face Leinad. "I have one remaining task, and my mission here will be complete, for a time. And yours will begin."

"My father spoke of a promise. What is the promise?" Leinad asked, resolving not to let Gabrik leave him with unanswered questions. How he would stop this massive warrior from leaving was something he wasn't sure how to accomplish.

Gabrik walked to the opposite side of his horse and removed an object. "The search for the promise begins with this, Leinad." Gabrik held forth the beautiful sword and scabbard Leinad and Peyton had seen in his blacksmith shop weeks earlier. "I was commissioned by the King to fashion it for you and deliver it today." The sword was truly a work of mastery. Leinad responded with disbelief and did not feel worthy to accept it.

"But I…I can't," Leinad said. "I am unable to—"

"You have been chosen, Leinad. If you do not accept the sword and its mission, the restoration of Arrethtrae may never come."

*I am but a boy,* Leinad thought. *I could not even save my father. Even with this magnificent sword, how can the King use the likes of me to bring restoration to the kingdom?* Leinad found a hundred reasons to refuse the sword and its mission, but one haunting truth would not let him: The King believed in him, and so did his father. Even if he failed, how could he deny such trust and honor?

Leinad stared at the sword offered to him and wondered at its beauty and purpose. He slowly lifted his hands to receive it.

"As the King lives, I swear to give Him my life in service."

Gabrik placed the sword in his hands, and Leinad secured the sword and scabbard about his waist. Strangely, it strengthened his heart and his resolve. He looked once again into the penetrating eyes of the Silent Warrior.

"What is the promise and where do I find it?"

Gabrik shook his head. "That is something I cannot answer, for I do not know."

"Then tell me, Gabrik…" Leinad hesitated before asking his next question. "Who is my brother?"

Gabrik paused, crossed his arms, and his gaze went to the ground. Leinad wondered what additional fabric of his life was about to be torn.

"We have urgent business to attend to, but you must know the answer to that question if you are to be prepared for what lies ahead. Before you were born, your mother gave birth to twin sons. Peyton raised them as he raised you. One son was a noble boy with a heart for the King. The other son, however, had a heart that would not be bridled, and his rebellious spirit directed him. His jealousy over his brother grew day by day. Your father loved them both, but all his efforts to turn the heart of the second son were met with contempt. One day, while in the fields away from your father, the second son's anger and jealousy became so great that he killed his brother."

Leinad now understood the ache he had felt in his mother's heart and the sense of failure he felt from his father from time to time. This was one of the lost pieces of the puzzle he had searched for regarding his own past.

"What happened to the—" Leinad spoke words that felt unfamiliar—"to my other brother?"

"He was banished from the region. The King ordered that he be given a wound across his forehead as punishment for his crime. He made his home in the distant land of Nod. Because of his skill with the sword, he was able to rise to a position of power and now commands a formidable army...an army of destruction."

As if a veil had been removed from his eyes, Leinad instantly made the connection of his brother's identity.

"His name is Zane!" he stated enthusiastically.

Gabrik raised one eyebrow. "Yes, how did you know?"

Leinad told Gabrik of his encounter with Lucius earlier that morning and also of his fight with the man named Zane. The realization that he had fought and nearly killed his brother gripped Leinad.

"Though Zane is a blood brother of yours," Gabrik said, "make no mistake about it—he is an enemy of the King and of the people of Arrethtrae. He will not hesitate to kill you or anyone else if that is what Lucius commands. Lucius will stop at nothing to disrupt the King's plan, and a man like Zane is a perfect tool." Gabrik continued to adjust the saddle and pack on his horse.

"Gabrik, why would a powerful warrior like Lucius need Zane to accomplish his work?"

Gabrik quickly set to removing his pack from his horse. "The King's Silent Warriors are Lucius's primary concern. The people of Arrethtrae are largely unaware of the ferocious battle that is occurring in their land between us and Lucius and his Shadow Warriors. The victor of the hidden war will rule Arrethtrae. Just as the King has chosen you as a key part in His plan to bring victory, Lucius has chosen your brother and his men to accomplish his evil purposes overtly. Now that Lucius has eliminated your father, he will use every resource available to him, including Zane, to widen his influence in the entire kingdom. He plans to rule Arrethtrae one day…and he is a patient man. If he knows of your existence, he will seek to destroy you as well. But do not fear, Leinad, the King will be with you in ways that you will not even realize."

Gabrik was nearly finished preparing his horse. "Leinad, the people of Kerr are in serious danger. By order of the King, you must ride to Mankin and warn the city of an approaching disaster. You must hurry."

"What disaster are you speaking of, Gabrik?"

Gabrik stopped his preparations and became very serious. "The Vactor Deluge."

Leinad looked at Tess, and her puzzled look mirrored his own confusion.

"The Vactor Deluge is a terror that is coming upon the land like no one has ever seen before," Gabrik said. "It is an innumerable swarm of miniature creatures called Vactors. They are so small that a grouping of thousands will darken only the tip of an arrow. Individually they are little more than a nuisance, but as a massive swarm that covers an entire countryside, they are devastating. Originating from the shores of the sea, they will devour the entire land. Any living substance, from the grass to the trees to the cattle to the people—all will be consumed. The swarm moves on the ground at a speed faster than a swift horse, without warning. There is no escape."

Had Leinad heard this from anyone other than Gabrik, he would have found it difficult to believe. But Gabrik's words were the King's words, so Leinad chose to believe.

"How can anyone survive such a terror?" he asked.

"You must get the people to high country. The Tara Hills Mountain Range will provide enough elevation to save them. The Vactors cannot survive in the heights of the mountains. Get yourselves and the people there, and you will live. Once the supply of food for the Vactors is exhausted, they will die, and the land will be reborn after some time has passed."

Leinad silently questioned himself and his capabilities. *This day is becoming a nightmare of nightmares...when will I awake?* His thoughts were interrupted by Gabrik's large hand on his shoulder.

"The King believes in you, Leinad. Now you must believe in the King and in the confidence He has in you."

It was the one and only moment of tenderness Leinad had ever seen in Gabrik. He returned the affirmation with a firm nod.

Gabrik quickly scanned the surrounding country. "Enough talk. We may be too late already. Lucius stole your horses, so you must take mine. It is time for me to rejoin my men."

Leinad mounted the large steed, and Gabrik effortlessly lifted Tess onto the saddle behind him. Leinad looked down at Gabrik as he stroked the horse's mane.

"What is his name?" Leinad asked.

"Deliverance."

"Will I see you again?" he asked of the mysterious companion who had been a friend and an unknown protector of Leinad and his father for many years.

Gabrik looked at Leinad but did not answer his question. "For the King's honor!" Then he turned and began jogging northward.

Leinad turned his horse and his thoughts toward Mankin. Even if he reached them in time, what could he say that would make them believe him?

Tess held Leinad's waist tightly as he pressed Deliverance into a full gallop and raced toward the unknown. As the wind blew across his face, Leinad wondered what path he should take. Deliverance instinctively knew the way to Mankin and followed it. Leinad was envious, for his course was unknown.

The familiarity of his farm quickly fell behind, and so did the life he once knew. Though his heart ached for what once was, in the depths of his soul he knew he would never be able to return.

## CHAPTER SIX

# LET
# THEM HEAR

Leinad and Tess made the ride to Mankin in record time but still arrived late in the afternoon. The town was in the midst of a wedding celebration complete with music, dancing, and much drinking. But a terrifying storm was building, and no one could see it. At the cursing of many, Leinad did not slow his horse until he reached the town square. He quickly dismounted and left Tess with Deliverance as he ran a few paces across the square platform to the bell tower and pulled the rope twice to signal a town meeting. He knew that he would lose time if the townspeople retreated to their homes under a full alarm. It would be necessary to convince them of the severity of the impending disaster. When the music stopped, the celebration quickly diminished.

The town prefect emerged from the courtyard of his manor house, which was near the edge of the town square, where the celebration seemed to be centered. As the prefect made his way to the bell tower, it was clear that he was extremely annoyed. A few of the prominent men of Mankin accompanied him. As they neared the bell tower and saw that the alarmist was a boy, their demeanor changed from annoyance to anger. Many of the people were already gathering at the platform where all of the meetings were held.

"What is the meaning of this, boy?" the prefect barked. "I am the only one in Mankin that can call a town meeting!"

"Prefect, I am Leinad, Peyton's son. I was sent by the King to warn you of a disaster that is coming to destroy Mankin."

The prefect burst into laughter. "If the King is still alive, He doesn't rule these parts. I am the authority here, and besides, there is no disaster coming that we have not already survived."

Although the smell of wine was heavy on his breath, he was well in control of his faculties, much to Leinad's amazement.

The people in the square moved from the prefect's manor across to the bell tower. Others outside the square joined them as well. The square was filling rapidly.

"Please, Prefect, there is not much time," Leinad said. "The King has told me to warn you of the Vactor Deluge. It will come from the coasts and devour everything in its path. You must warn the people and tell them to flee to the hills and hide until this passes."

"Listen here, boy!" the prefect said. "I govern these people, and nobody tells me what to do! I have no reason to believe anything you have said. And as far as the King is concerned, if He even exists, we run things our way."

By now the square was full. Leinad knew that the prefect would not listen, so he risked offending him further by addressing the people directly.

"People of Mankin!" Leinad shouted to reach the entire crowd with his words.

"Seize him!" the prefect shouted to his aids.

Leinad knew he had but one chance. "This morning my father was murdered by the Dark Knight!"

The approaching men and the crowd fell silent and still. It gave Leinad the opportunity he needed. However, the message he delivered was hard to speak, and the emotions began to swell within him as he thought of his father.

"The Dark Knight is a myth!" a man shouted from the crowd.

"No!" Leinad said. "I have seen him with my own eyes! He is very real and every bit as vicious as the stories portray. Though he is evil and powerful, even he was preparing to leave this land because of the devastation that is about to occur. Your lives and your children's lives are at stake! You must flee to the hills if you want to live. The Vactor Deluge is coming and will devour every living thing in its path, including you. It may be approaching the city even as we speak. You must believe me!"

The silence that followed Leinad's urgent warning slowly became a low rumble of indistinguishable voices.

The prefect stepped forward. "People, people! Have I ever allowed this community to be harmed in the past? No, of course not." He quickly answered his own question. "How many of you have ever heard of such a thing as these Vactor creatures?" He paused and scanned the crowd. "That's what

I thought. Well, neither have I. This morning we awoke and began celebrating a wedding. Tonight we will continue that celebration on into tomorrow. This boy is trying to frighten you into leaving Mankin and all of your belongings behind. How do we know he is not part of a band of thieves that will rob you once you've left? Do not worry. Life will continue as it always has."

Leinad felt the people slipping into apathetic disbelief. "If you do not leave the town now, you will die! This warning is from the King Himself." Leinad felt as if he were trying to warn a sleeping drunk of an approaching flash flood.

"How do we know it's from the King?" shouted another man from the crowd.

"Yes!" exclaimed another. "Give us proof, and we will believe you."

Leinad hung his head, closed his eyes, and clenched his jaw in frustration. How could he possibly prove that he was a messenger of the King?

The crowd began to murmur again. He heard sporadic ridiculing laughter, and he felt like a fool. He began to question himself.

*Maybe this* is *all a big hoax after all,* he thought. *I haven't seen the King either.* Leinad opened his eyes and saw the gallant sword within its scabbard at his side.

"I will give you a sign that what I am telling you is indeed from the King," he said boldly.

He withdrew the magnificent sword and held it high above his head, showing all the people the insignia of the king in the pommel. The crowd hushed again to silence and stared in awe at the beautiful sword.

"This proves nothing!" the prefect shouted. "We all have seen swords as splendid as this one even among the thieves that raid us. Be gone from us, boy, and take your pretty little sword with you!"

Some of the crowd began to jeer at Leinad. Soon the entire mass of people had turned their backs on Leinad and the warning he carried. The sword slowly descended and came to rest limply at Leinad's side.

"Get out of my town, boy!" The prefect glared at Leinad, then turned and proceeded back to his manor house with his consorts close behind. "Let the celebration continue!" he yelled, and music filled the air once again.

Leinad felt as though he had disgraced himself and the King by failing to convince the people of the impending danger. Anger, frustration, and humiliation incapacitated him. He sheathed the sword and sat down on the edge of the platform with his head buried in his hands. There was no energy or desire within him to carry on. He had lost his father. He had failed the King. It was a day that was bigger than he was, and he accepted defeat in his heart. The moments passed, and the sun settled on the horizon as a flood of disaster approached—and he didn't care.

"Why did I even try to warn these foolish people," he said out loud to himself. "Not even one of them believed me."

"I believe you, Leinad." The small tender voice of Tess was accompanied by a gentle hand on his shoulder.

It startled Leinad, for he thought he was alone. He turned and looked up into the face of his young friend...his only friend. Like a slap across the face, he was reminded of the responsibility that had become buried in his own self-pity.

"Tess! What am I doing?" he exclaimed. "I've got to get you out of here! Where's Deliverance?"

"I tied 'im up over yonder by the tower," she said and pointed to the bell tower.

He quickly gained his feet and faced her. "Good thinking, Tess. Come on."

He grabbed her hand and ran to the waiting horse. The door of escape was closing quickly. He mounted the horse and then reached down to lift her onto the saddle behind him.

"Hang on, Tess. We've got no time to waste."

Tess wrapped her arms around Leinad's waist and placed her face against his back. Leinad kicked the haunches of the horse and rode toward the rugged terrain of the Tara Hills Mountain Range that lay southeast of Mankin. Leinad was thankful they lay in the opposite direction of the sea.

On any other day, the mountains appeared to be close to the town, but today they seemed a far too distant destination. The plain that spanned the gap between the town and the mountains was flat and lush with tall grass and an occasional grouping of trees. Leinad paced his horse just shy of a full gallop, for though they had covered half the journey, he knew the climb up the mountains would be exhausting for Deliverance.

"Leinad," Tess said fearfully, "look!" She pointed back toward Mankin.

The front wave of a dark and ominous mass was moving toward the city. An eerie orange mist trailing the Vactor Deluge caught the rays of the setting sun to paint an alien landscape never before seen in the kingdom.

Leinad heard the fear in Tess's voice and felt it through the embrace around his waist. He fought back the apprehension that was rising within him. There was no rescue and no escape for the people now.

Leinad was amazed at the speed of the Vactor creatures. As the edge of the mass hit Mankin, the distant screams of the people beckoned to Leinad and Tess, but they did not last long. Within moments the Vactor Deluge encircled and overran what was once a celebratory town. Two or three men on horses tried to escape, but it was a feeble attempt. Leinad pressed Deliverance into a full gallop and focused on the ground before him.

"Hurry, Leinad…hurry! It's gainin' on us!" Tess's voice was trembling, which did not help Leinad fight back the panic that threatened to swallow him.

The horse beneath them seemed to feel the urgency as well and reached further with each stride. The beast was sweating profusely, and Leinad wondered if there would be anything left in him once they reached the mountains.

The Vactor Deluge had already covered over half the distance between Leinad and Tess and what was once the town. Although the sun was nearly set, the remnant ambient light was bright enough for Leinad to chart their course. It also revealed the approaching darkness beneath the rising orange cloud of the Vactor Deluge.

As they approached the rugged terrain of the Tara Hills, Leinad did not pause to route their ascent. He let Deliverance choose the path of least resistance. "Attaboy, Deliverance. We're almost there." He patted the steed's wet hide.

"Are we gonna make it, Leinad?" Tess asked.

"We're going to make it, Tess. Just you wait and see."

"But it's movin' so fast!" she exclaimed and pointed to the ferocious mass that was now three-fourths of the way across the plain.

"We'll make it," Leinad said to assure both of them.

He urged Deliverance farther into the foothills and up the mountains, away from destruction. He wondered how high they must climb to escape the encroaching horror. The ascent seemed agonizingly slow compared to the pace they were used to crossing the plain.

The Vactor Deluge reached the foothills, and the base trees disappeared beneath the black mass. Leinad focused on one large group of trees, which slowly collapsed until there was nothing.

Deliverance hesitated at a steep rise in their path. The beast was nearly spent and began to stumble occasionally, but Leinad had no choice but to push him onward. Leinad figured the Vactor Deluge would be upon them soon. There was little time left.

A bizarre sound accompanied the eerie orange mist that seemed to rise from the consuming mass. It sounded to Leinad like a million twigs were being stepped on at the same time. It was a sound that grew louder and louder. Leinad's mind begged for it to stop—but it would not be stopped.

*How high…? How high must we climb?* Leinad asked himself.

As the Vactor Deluge approached, its speed was even more evident. The rise in terrain did not slow it like it did their horse. Deliverance stumbled and nearly fell. His panting was deep and rapid.

"Here it comes, Leinad! What are we going to do?"

Leinad kicked Deliverance to climb the rise in front of them, and the powerful muscles moved them forward one more time. Up...up...up. The noise was incessant, and the rising orange mist had a sharp odor that penetrated their nostrils.

The Vactor Deluge was upon them.

An outcrop of rocks formed a ledge and was just a few paces before them. Leinad directed Deliverance to it. Tess could not take her eyes off the enveloping dark mass as it quickly overtook them. Deliverance could go no more.

"Stand up and jump to the rocks, Tess!" Leinad shouted.

She steadied herself by holding on to Leinad's shoulders and jumped to the rock ledge above them. The Vactor creatures reached the hooves of the horse and enveloped his legs.

"Keep climbing, Tess! Keep climbing!"

"Jump, Leinad!" Tess screamed.

Deliverance neighed wildly and bit at the vicious mass moving up his body. Leinad stood and nearly fell for the shaking of the steed under its pain. The horse became a moving black

© Marcella Johnson

mass, and Leinad jumped as Deliverance fell to the ground in agony. Having lost some of his momentum from the horse's fall, Leinad landed short of his target and hung on the rock ledge with his feet dangling below. Some of the Vactor creatures had reached his feet before he jumped, and Leinad felt the leather of his shoes fall away. Instantly, he felt as though his feet were on fire. The pain nearly caused him to lose his grip, but Tess reached for him.

"C'mon, Leinad! Climb!" She pulled on his arms, and he swung his body up and over the rock ledge.

He rolled into a sitting position, and his only thought was to stop the fire on his feet. They were bare and covered in the blackness of the Vactors. He fervently brushed his ankles and feet.

"Go, Tess! Before it reaches this ledge!" he shouted above the noise of the Vactor Deluge.

"Look at your feet. It ain't movin' up your legs like it did to Deliverance!" she exclaimed above the noise.

Leinad noticed that the black mass that was once on his feet lay on the ground in a near motionless, powdery heap. Though his feet were red and tender, they were still there.

Leinad stood, and Tess grabbed his arm. She was shaking, and Leinad placed his arm around her to steady her. They looked out over the ledge to find that the dark mass of the Vactor Deluge rose no higher than just a few feet below them.

Leinad gazed over the once beautiful, lush countryside now blanketed with a black mass and a rising orange mist. There was nothing familiar about it now. It was a desert of unrecognizable blackness. The noise of the Vactor Deluge seemed to subside slightly with each passing moment.

"Poor Deliverance." Tess was staring down at the small mound of moving blackness beneath them.

"He was a noble steed. He delivered us, Tess. He gave his all and delivered us."

As Leinad scanned the horizon in the final moments of day, he thought of the future—their future and the kingdom's future. *Who will be noble enough to deliver us from the clutches of the Dark Knight?* he wondered.

"Come on, Tess. I want to put a little more distance between us and the Vactors before nightfall."

## CHAPTER SEVEN

# NO PLACE
# A HOME

 The Plains of Kerr was a no-man's-land as far as the eye could see. In the early morning light, Leinad could make out the distinct elevation line of the Vactor Deluge's destruction in the jagged profile of the Tara Hills Mountain Range. The night had been cool, and both he and Tess were looking forward to the shadows of the mountains disappearing and bringing some warmth to the air.

The sound of the Vactor Deluge was gone. It had slowly diminished through the night until silence once more filled the air. Leinad deduced that the Vactor Deluge had run its course and that it was probably safe to descend, but there was no point. There was nothing to descend to. The only life in the region, maybe in the entire kingdom for all Leinad knew, was above the Vactor Deluge's consumption line. He contemplated what to do next.

Tess was shivering. Leinad put his arm around her to warm her a bit and was thankful that her shaking was from the cool air and not from the previous night's terror. Leinad was proud of her for not losing her head in the whole ordeal. She was a tough little girl. He knew that the coming days of survival might be a lot worse if she was not as emotionally strong as she was. Leinad wasn't much more than a boy himself, but he knew he had to become a man…quickly. The responsibility of providing for and protecting Tess pushed him out of the selfishness and self-pity he was tempted to fall into.

Leinad's next move was dictated by the hunger pangs they were feeling. "Well, Tess," Leinad said, "I have a feeling that our breakfast is going to be pretty slim this morning."

"What do we do now, Leinad?" Tess asked. "We ain't got no food, no horse, an' no place to go."

"For now, Tess, there is only one thing we can do—survive!" Leinad managed a weak smile to encourage her.

"I know how ta survive on the streets in a town, but there ain't no town no more."

"The way I see it, we can't stay here forever. We know that the Plains of Kerr are not an option, so our only choice is to get to the other side of these mountains and see if some parts of the kingdom were unaffected by the Vactor Deluge."

"But you don't even have shoes, an' what are we gonna eat? You ain't gonna catch much with that sword."

Leinad raised an eyebrow. "That's for sure. It's going to take a few days to get prepared before we can even think about traveling. The first thing we need to do is find a water supply and hopefully a few berries to eat. Then we need to build a shelter and set up camp. Once we get that done, I'll focus on hunting up some meat for us."

Tess seemed to feel better having heard Leinad's plan.


WITHIN TWO DAYS, LEINAD and Tess had found a mountain stream that carried cold, fresh water to the desolate plains below them. They built a makeshift shelter nearby using logs, leaves, and grass. Although it was rather crude, it gave them some protection from the elements and afforded a feeling of security. Unfortunately, Leinad's plan to find game for food was more of a challenge than he'd expected. By the fifth day, Tess was so weak that she could not rise from her grassy bed. Leinad was weak himself, but the thought of failing Tess drove him to his feet. He made sure Tess had water and was warm.

"You rest, Tess," he said tenderly. "Today I will bring back some food."

Tess managed a weak smile but did not move or speak.

Without the means or time to make a decent bow, Leinad's hunting gear was comprised of three sharpened sticks to use as spears. He thought some animals must have been frightened to higher ground by the Vactor Deluge. The notion of climbing higher into the mountains in his weakened state was not pleasant, but he knew that Tess might not make it if he wasn't successful today. He climbed, listened, watched, and climbed some more. The flutter of a small bird was his only reward.

By midday, the sun was hot, and the physical and emotional strain was taking its toll on Leinad. He climbed a small rise that was much more difficult than it should have been and knelt down in a small clearing to catch his breath.

The frustration of an unfruitful hunt and the thought of returning to Tess empty-handed to watch her wither further was becoming unbearable. Leinad's thoughts turned to the past, where his father and their farm still remained on the fertile Plains of Kerr. His deep breaths became moans of despair, and he could not stop the tears that fell for the loss of joy that had embraced him just a few short days ago. Leinad had never had a chance to fully mourn for his father, and now the tremendous burden of being responsible for the life of another was overwhelming. He dropped his spears, fell to both knees, and covered his face with his hands. In the solitude of the mountain clearing, he wept.

"I have failed Tess, my father, my people, and my King. I can't do this," he whispered. "I can't do this!" he screamed and fell to the ground in the fetal position. He lay still and wept until a fitful sleep overcame his exhaustion and despair.


LEINAD WAS VAGUELY AWARE of the shadow that crossed his face and wondered if he had slept so long that the evening sun was already casting its long shadows from the trees.

"Leinad," came a strong but gentle voice from above him.

Leinad blinked groggily thinking he didn't remember voices sounding so real in his other dreams.

"Leinad. Wake up," said the voice again.

Leinad raised himself on one arm and looked up at the figure that was casting the shadow across him. A man with broad shoulders and a noble face stood before him. Across his shoulders was a young antlered deer. He dropped the game to the ground and knelt down to Leinad.

Leinad wiped his eyes and wondered if his weakened condition was causing his mind to hallucinate. "Who are you?" he managed to ask.

"Here…drink some water," the stranger said as he put a flask of water to Leinad's lips.

He drank heavily.

"You must eat, but eat slowly and not too much," he said, offering some sweet bread and a bit of dried meat.

It took a tremendous amount of discipline not to devour the food ravenously, for it was delicious. Leinad immediately thought of Tess.

"I have to get this to Tess," he said earnestly and began to rise.

The stranger put a firm hand on his shoulder. "We will get to her soon, but you must take another minute to eat and strengthen yourself."

Leinad stopped and looked into the eyes of the stranger for the first time. They were penetrating eyes, and yet they held the same love that he remembered seeing in his father's eyes. He was handsome and carried himself as a nobleman.

"Who are you, sir?" Leinad asked again.

"I am a man from a distant land."

Leinad thought that he looked more like a prince than a traveler. He finished his meat and drank again.

"Thank you for your kindness, sir. We are in a desperate situation, and I must get food to my friend back at camp," Leinad said.

"Yes, I know. Let us make haste and get Tess some food."

His tone made Leinad feel as though this man knew Tess. He seemed to know Leinad as well, but he was sure he had never seen the man before.

The stranger helped Leinad to his feet and easily lifted the young buck back onto his shoulders. They hurried back to Leinad's campsite.

When they arrived, Tess was barely coherent. Leinad fed her some of the sweet bread and water and let her rest again.

"It will take you a few days to nurse her back to full strength." The stranger looked down at her and smiled. "She has a good heart, Leinad. Take care of her." It was more than a request; it was a charge. "I will leave the rest of my provisions with you. Take the deer, and cook what you need. Dry the rest of the meat to take on your journey."

This man and his knowledge of their condition perplexed Leinad, but there was a natural authority in him that brought comfort.

"Can you travel with us, sir?" Leinad asked hopefully.

"I'm sorry, Leinad, that is not possible. You must make this journey on your own. My path lies in a different direction."

Leinad looked down toward the ground. His confidence in his own abilities was waning. A gleam of sunlight caught his eye as it reflected off a magnificent sword that hung at the stranger's side. It was a sword that had no equal. The mark on the sword was the same as the one on his sword—the mark of the King.

The stranger placed his hand on Leinad's shoulder. "You have done well, Leinad. Do not be afraid or discouraged. The King will be with you. Your calling is noble, and you are well suited to fulfill it."

Leinad looked up into the stranger's eyes once again and found the confidence that had left him. "What am I supposed to do?"

"You must travel south to the Valley of Nan. Those people have been chosen by the King to fulfill his plan for Arrethtrae."

Leinad nodded. "I will do as the King wishes."

The stranger smiled, looked toward Tess, and left their campsite in a northerly direction.

With the provisions left behind by the stranger, Leinad and Tess regained their strength over the next few days. Leinad decided to travel around the mountains just above the Vactor Deluge consumption line on their journey to the Valley of Nan. He did not want to risk crossing over the mountains with the cold season approaching. As they moved south, they became more adept at locating food, though there seemed to be no end to the destruction of the Vactor Deluge. Their progress was slow but steady. Most of their energy was spent on surviving and traveling. A mutual respect grew out of the enormity of their challenge.

After many weeks of travel, they finally reached the southern portion of the Tara Hills Mountain Range. The aftermath of the Vactor Deluge was still evident clear up to the Red Canyon, which lay a day's journey across what once was a fertile plain. By midday one afternoon, they had reached a vantage point that enabled them to see far to the south.

"Look beyond the canyon, Tess," Leinad said. "What do you see?"

Tess strained her eyes, for the distance was great and the horizon was slightly hazy. "It looks like…green!" she exclaimed.

They both smiled for the first time in many days.

"Yes. Green!" Leinad said. "And that's where we're headed as soon as we can stock up on food and water to make it across that barren plain. We'd better plan on two days of provisions."

Once they were ready, they descended to the Vactor Deluge consumption line. They stopped just a few feet above the motionless black mass. Being this close to the Vactor creatures, even though they were dead, made Leinad and Tess uneasy. The disturbing memories of that sorrowful day a few weeks earlier flooded back into Leinad's mind.

He reached down with the tip of the hunting bow he had fashioned and pushed some of the mass aside. To his surprise, the bow uncovered the tender spires of thick, fresh grass growing beneath.

"Look, Tess," he said. "It's lush too. It's as though the soil is more fertile than it was before."

He stepped onto the black mass and felt the cushion of the grass. It was a strange sensation standing on the dark mass that earlier had ravaged the countryside.

He reached out for Tess's hand. "Come on, Sunshine. Let's go find a home."

Tess smiled and obliged.

The journey across the plain was not pleasant. Their clothes were soon covered from the waist down with a black powder. They were careful not to stir up the mass, but it was nearly impossible. They were forced to cover their mouths with a cloth to improve the air they breathed. Leinad decided to travel on through the night and into the next day if need be. The thought of sleeping in the black powder was unacceptable to him.

Leinad and Tess were grateful to finally reach the majestic Red Canyon. However, it posed a formidable task to cross, as the canyon was enormous. The reddish rocks and soil added to the impression that it was a scar that ran from the Great Sea deep into the heart of the kingdom. Leinad could see that the river that flowed on the canyon floor was the dividing line between land consumed by the Vactor Deluge and land that was still alive.

The sights below as they stood on the ridge above the canyon nearly took their breath away. Descending the canyon walls would be treacherous, and there was no going around it. On the opposite side of the canyon, Leinad could see a long, narrow tributary that branched from the main gorge in a southwest direction, where the canyon floor rose to meet the green plains beyond, but there was no such tributary on this side.

Leinad and Tess traveled along the canyon's rim until they found a portion of the steep wall they felt they could negotiate. After many hours of careful but exhausting work, they set foot on the canyon floor. They rinsed themselves in the river and were glad to be rid of the black dust that clung to their skin and clothes. The swim was refreshing, and they would have lingered, but exhaustion overcame them. They crossed the river and set foot on level ground untouched by the Vactor Deluge. In the shade of the canyon walls, they slept.

Leinad and Tess traveled east on the canyon floor until they found a way to ascend the steep walls and enter the land they had spotted from the mountains.

After a few more days of traveling, they entered the Valley of Nan. The land was foreign, but the sight of farms in the distance renewed their spirits. The valley was not particularly lush, but it was fertile enough to support the many farms that dotted the countryside. They were anxious to meet people, but Leinad had to remind himself and Tess to be cautious.

They stood on a rise that looked over the valley. It was the first time in many weeks that both of them felt joyful. Leinad breathed deeply, and Tess raised both of her arms into the air as if to hug the whole valley.

"We made it, Sunshine," Leinad said with a sigh.

Tess hugged Leinad's arm and smiled. "We made it," she echoed.

## CHAPTER EIGHT

# BETRAYED!

 Not knowing the disposition of the people, and not wanting to draw undue attention to himself in an exclusively farming region, Leinad felt it was necessary to temporarily hide his sword and blend in with the people. He wrapped it in deer hide and buried it beneath a large stone near a grove of trees at the edge of the valley.

The people in the Valley of Nan were kind but not necessarily warm in their greetings. Leinad learned later that their hesitant kindness was because of the raids that had occurred in times past. In other regions of the kingdom, castle lords were often in need of slaves to work their land and their castles. The Valley of Nan was one of many regions targeted to supply this labor. Most of the farms in the valley were extremely functional and simple. The people were independent and yet loyal to one another. There was no established government or elected leader. However, the size of a farm established prominence, and Master Stanton was by far the most prominent man in the region.

Leinad and Tess were offered a meal and a barn to sleep in by a family on the fringe of the valley. The extra burden was more than they could ask of the family for more than one night, however, and Leinad knew he must find a farm that would hire, feed, and lodge the both of them for a time. Thus he was directed to Master Stanton.

As they entered Master Stanton's land the next day and approached the farm, Leinad heard a strong voice barking commands to servants and farmhands. Two large men with pitchforks approached them.

"This is Master Stanton's land, and he doesn't want any trespassers," one of the men said.

Leinad held up his hands to show them empty. "We enter peacefully and come only to seek work on Master Stanton's farm."

This answer seemed to satisfy the burly men, and Leinad and Tess were escorted to the front of the large farmhouse, where Stanton was still giving orders for the day. Leinad and Tess waited patiently and listened. Stanton seemed to be a harsh man, but the people that had provided lodging the previous night said he was a fair man…in most situations. When the orders were complete, Leinad and Tess stepped forward to introduce themselves.

"Master Stanton," Leinad said with all politeness, "I am Leinad, and this is my friend Tess. We have traveled a great distance and are looking for work in exchange for food and lodging. It is our understanding that your farm and land are the finest around. Would you be so kind, sir, as to tell us if you are in need of some extra help?"

Stanton's face was leathery from the endless days of labor in the sun. It appeared to Leinad that this man worked as hard as if not harder than any of his servants. His hands were large, brown, and strong. He scrutinized Leinad and Tess with pursed lips and squinted eyes.

"Where are you from, son?" he asked.

Leinad relaxed slightly. "We are from the Plains of Kerr, across the Red Canyon to the north, sir."

"Do you know anything about farming?"

"It is what I have spent my entire life doing," Leinad said with a bit of pride.

Stanton continued his scrutiny of the two strangers a few moments longer. "I'll give you food and lodging for a hard day's work, and the little miss can work in the kitchen with the other servant girls. Once I see how you do, we'll talk about wages. Fair enough?"

Leinad smiled and nodded. "Thank you, sir. You will not be disappointed with our work."

"I'd better not be," Stanton stated abruptly. He then softened slightly. "Go to the kitchen and get some biscuits and water. Once you've eaten, report to Supervisor Benreu in the west fields. Tess, Mrs. Stanton will tell you what she needs done."

"Yes, sir," they replied in unison.

THE NEXT FEW WEEKS WERE a time of adjustment. The work was hard, but it was a relief not to have to worry about where the next meal was coming from. They were both quartered in barrack houses built for the workers. Leinad found an opportunity to retrieve his sword and hid it beneath a loose floorboard in the barrack house he was assigned to. He enjoyed working the land again. It reminded him of his father and the joyful days on his own farm. If Leinad was apprehensive about anything, it was his supervisor, Benreu. Leinad did not care for him nor did he trust him. The other six men under him were crude men with a clear loyalty to Benreu. Leinad was glad that Tess was working in the farmhouse away from these brutes.

The west fields were over a knoll and beyond the sight of the Stanton farm. A road ran nearby that connected the Valley of Nan with the other regions in the kingdom. On an overcast afternoon, Leinad glanced up from his work to see a caravan of carts and horses approaching from the east. All work stopped, and the other workers looked as if they recognized the caravan.

"Who are they?" Leinad asked the nearest farmhand.

The man looked at Leinad and responded with a crooked smile. The other hands had worked their way close to Leinad.

"Grab him!" Benreu shouted.

The men bound Leinad with rope and hauled him to the roadside. Leinad wondered what his fate would be. A deal was quickly struck, and Leinad was placed in a caged cart in exchange for a bag of money.

The caravan leader, obviously an acquaintance of Benreu, appeared in a hurry to be on his way, but Benreu halted him. He walked to the work wagon and recovered something wrapped in cloth. He returned to the caravan and displayed Leinad's sword.

"How much for this elegant sword?" he asked the caravan leader.

Leinad was shocked that Benreu had found his sword. *He must have planned this for a long time,* Leinad thought.

A second deal was struck concerning the sword. Leinad found himself a prisoner, without his sword, on a road that led to a foreign destination. He wondered if he would ever see Tess again. Surely this wasn't part of the King's plan. A familiar despair fell upon his heart. The kingdom seemed so big and chaotic. He wondered if the King was big enough to rule such a land. It was overwhelming for a boy to contemplate, for he felt as insignificant as a pebble on the beach.

The caravan made two more stops for merchandise trades and slave purchases before arriving in the region of Nyland three days later. Nyland was lush and beautiful, but Leinad was so sore from the bumps and bruises of the journey that he hardly noticed. He was thankful that the journey was almost over, no matter where it ended. The caravan made its way through a large grove of trees and on toward a prominent castle that sprawled across the crest of a hill. It was a magnificent castle. Leinad had never seen such a bold structure that integrated beauty and strength so perfectly.

"Pyron Mid," said one of the other captives.

"What?" Leinad asked.

"Pyron Mid. The castle is called Pyron Mid. Haven't you ever heard of it?"

"No. Should I have?"

"Lord Fairos's Pyron Mid is the grandest castle in all the land, and its mortar is the sweat and blood of the hundreds of slaves he keeps."

The castle was massive, with walls that towered above the landscape. A moat encircled the castle, as well as additional land to allow for future expansion. On their approach, Leinad saw people working the numerous fields. The soil looked dark and fertile.

Once the caravan came to a halt, Leinad and the other captives were lined up outside the castle walls. They waited until a sturdy man dressed in the apparel of a knight rode across the drawbridge upon a splendid gray steed.

"Ah, Lord Fairos," the caravan leader exclaimed. "It is truly a pleasure to see you. I trust your recent conquests have been profitable for you?"

"Cut the drivel, Dagon," Lord Fairos said. "What have you got?"

"I have a fine selection of the very best slaves available for you to choose from today."

Fairos did not dismount. He circled the six captives from his mount, inspecting each one. He stopped in front of them. "Which of you have laid brick and mortar?"

No one responded.

He turned to Dagon. "You know what I need, Dagon. Why do you keep bringing incompetents that I must train before they are useful to me?"

"Sire, sire," Dagon said in a tone that was slightly patronizing, "what you need is not readily available in the kingdom. But what I have brought you are six strong backs. They will be productive for you within a day…that is a promise from Dagon."

Fairos eyed the lineup once again. "Very well. But if any falter within a month, you will return my money. Is that clear?"

"Of course, my lord. Of course."

Fairos turned to the captives once again. "You are mine now. You will work hard and long. In return I will feed you and let you live. If you try to run, my men will hunt you down and kill you. I give no second chances. Do you understand?"

A couple of the men nodded slowly, but Fairos did not wait for a reply. "Dagon, take them to the west wall, and turn them over to my guards. Afterward you may see my treasury officer to collect the usual fee."

"Yes, Lord Fairos. It's been a pleasure doing business with you."

Fairos turned his horse and galloped into the country.

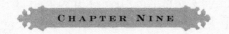

CHAPTER NINE

# BEGINNING OF BONDAGE

Leinad was one of many slaves in Nyland. The other men, women, and children that made up Lord Fairos's labor force came from all over the kingdom. Slave traders like Dagon frequented the castle, and occasionally Lord Fairos's own forces would raid other lands and bring the spoils, including slaves, back to the castle.

In his loneliness, Leinad's thoughts often turned to Tess. He was thankful that she was with the Stantons, for he believed they were good people, but he missed her. Only now did he realize what a friend that little girl had become. Her cheerful, freckled face made him smile when he thought of her.

Leinad continually thought of escaping, but the slaves were under constant guard. One of the new slaves did attempt an escape, but his flight was short and his execution quick. All of the slaves were forced to watch. Lord Fairos used it as an example of what would happen to anyone else who might make a similar attempt. It was an effective deterrent, but it did not stop Leinad from planning. He knew that he would just have to be extremely prepared and careful when the opportunity arrived.

Not many weeks passed before another slave trader arrived with over twenty new slaves. Leinad saw the arrival of the caravan and wondered what new stories of woe would accompany its occupants. From his vantage point on the west wall, he could just see the lineup and Lord Fairos's inspection. The distance was too far to see any details, but he was able to discern that it was a mix of adults and children, probably the result of a village raid.

"Get back to work, slave!" ordered a nearby overseer. A whip cracked, but not upon any flesh...this time. The overseers were Nylanders that Fairos put over the slaves to prevent escape and to "encourage" them to work efficiently. That encouragement usually came as the uninhibited use of their whips.

Leinad resumed his labor but kept his eye on the new arrivals across the moat. The negotiations finished, and the new slaves were marched across the drawbridge. Their shoulders were slumped and their heads hung low, all except one youngster in the middle. The confident posture was familiar to Leinad. *Tess, could it be you?* He did not dare hope that his young friend would suffer his same demise, but he couldn't deny a lift in his spirits. He missed her companionship in this lonely place. Leinad worked and watched while he wondered where they would be stationed.

The guards met the slave trader and his captives once they crossed the drawbridge and proceeded to direct them to the west wall. This side of the castle expansion was massive, with hundreds of slaves working the bricks. The guards all carried swords as their main weapon of influence, while the overseers preferred whips. As the line of slaves proceeded, overseers chose the slaves they wanted to do the work they were responsible for. Naturally, the largest males were taken first, and the numbers dwindled quickly as they approached Leinad's section of the wall. A few older females and the youth were left now as they passed the overseer responsible for Leinad and the slaves around him.

"How do you expect me to get any work done on this blasted wall if all you bring me are old women and children?" the overseer said.

"From what I've seen, these old biddies outperform the men half the time, so quit your gripin'," the guard replied. "Do you want them or not?"

Leinad recognized Tess and wanted to shout for her, but he restrained himself. Tess, however, did not restrain herself once she recognized Leinad.

"Leinad!" she exclaimed as she bolted from the line and ran to him.

Leinad dropped his work and ran to meet her. He knew there would be repercussions now anyway, so he wanted to be the bearer of any pain that might come.

"Back in line, slave!" the guard shouted, and he drew his sword as he pursued her.

Leinad quickened his pace to close the distance between them. Tess reached him and hugged his waist tightly. He returned the hug, then said in a hushed voice, "Don't say a word."

The guard reached them and drew back his sword. Leinad put Tess behind him and faced the guard.

"I am sorry, sir," Leinad said. "We are friends and haven't seen each other for a very long time. Please do not harm her. She is just a girl."

The guard hesitated, and then lowered his sword. "Back in line, slave. If you ever break line again, I will cut you in two."

The overseer joined them, and Leinad said to him, "Sir, I can vouch for the ability of this girl. She works as hard as any man twice her size. To have her on your line will be a tremendous asset to you."

The overseer looked skeptical. "Let me see you, slave," he snarled at Tess.

She stepped out from behind Leinad, straightened her back, and lifted her chin. Such a response from an adult slave would have brought an instant whipping.

"She is but a girl. How much work could I possibly get out of her?"

"Give her one week, sir, and you will be impressed. I promise," Leinad said.

"She's small, but she's got spunk. You train her, but you'd better be right or you'll both pay." The overseer turned to the guard. "Take the old women to Lady Fairos. Maybe she needs them in the kitchens. I don't want any more lame workers here."

The guard and the overseer left to resume their duties.

Leinad turned to Tess and grabbed her shoulders. "Hello, Sunshine." He smiled bigger than he had in months.

She smiled back and threw her arms around him again.

He returned the hug and then moved them back to the wall. "What happened, Tess? How did you end up here?"

"Raiders attacked the Stanton farm. Master Stanton got killed…most of the folks was killed. I hid 'neath the farmhouse steps. They was mean people, Leinad. They just wanted ta kill people and steal things." Tess looked down at the ground somberly as she recalled the horror of that night for Leinad.

"Did you get hurt?" Leinad asked.

"No, but I's lucky to be alive, Leinad. Lots a people died that night… It was horrible."

"Who were these raiders, Tess?"

"I don't know, but they was mean and gross lookin' too."

"Did they ever find you?" Leinad asked.

"No. I stayed hid till they left. Later, when I was scroungin' for food, a slave trader saw me and brought me here." She looked back up at Leinad. "I's so glad to be here with you, Leinad, even if I is a slave." She smiled again.

Leinad put his arm around her shoulder. "I'm sorry I wasn't there to protect you, Tess, but I'm glad you're all right. And it sure is good to see you too." He smiled back at his young friend. *It doesn't seem quite so lonely anymore,* he thought.

And it wasn't.

## CHAPTER TEN

# MASTERY UNVEILED

Life for Leinad and Tess was hard, but Fairos did feed them well. Leinad assumed it was because he knew that productive work depended on it. Fairos was the most powerful and influential man in this region of Arrethtrae, and he intended to expand his realm as far as possible. Of course, the icon of power was the magnificence of one's castle. Therefore, the labor of most of the servants, including Leinad and Tess, was the same every day—expand the size of the castle. Fairos hired a master mason and those with experience in building marvelous structures and buildings, but the heavy labor was accomplished by the slaves

Leinad and Tess worked side by side most days, and as the months wore on, he became more than a big brother to her. He felt responsible for protecting her, for watching over her, and for teaching her. Their friendship grew out of a need for companionship during difficult days. Each day, Leinad tried to impart some of the same instruction he had received from his father, and Tess responded with enthusiasm. It broke the drudgery of the day.

Over time, Leinad could see that the rough edges of this abandoned, wounded little girl were beginning to smooth and heal in spite of the long hard days of servitude. He taught her about the King and His promise for a just and honorable kingdom. He helped her understand the virtues of honesty, loyalty, integrity, and commitment. Even her speech became more proper and refined, although there were many days that Leinad nearly gave up, for this was the most difficult lesson of all for her.

Fairos spent much of his time planning the expansion of the territory of Nyland, but he also loved the challenge of a good sword fight. He was very skilled with the sword. He practiced occasionally with his castle guards, but oftentimes he wanted the thrill of a real fight. It was at these times that he called for his guards to pick two or three slaves and bring them to his courtyard, arm them with swords, and he would fight them all at once. The slaves dreaded those days, for whoever was chosen would be wounded or maimed, sometimes even killed, in the fight.

Today was such a day.

Leinad and Tess were working on the west wall of the new section of the castle. The crisp, blue morning had yielded to a hot, muggy afternoon. Overseers were walking the work line.

Leinad was struggling with an oppressive spirit, and though he tried to hide it from Tess, he was sure she could sense it.

"Great day to build a castle, aye, Leinad?" Tess said with a grin.

Leinad looked at the dirty, sweat-soaked face of his young friend and managed a weak smile. She was always the one to encourage him.

"Yes, Sunshine," he said with an edge of sarcasm in his voice as he handed her a large brick. "A mighty fine day indeed." More and more, Leinad took to affectionately calling her Sunshine. The name reminded him of his father.

Tess took the brick from him, and he tried to lift his own spirits with some teasing. "It's like a friend once told me: 'It's importin' ta looks on the bright sides o' things.'"

Tess responded with a smirk and a glare from the corner of her eye as she hoisted the brick into place.

"You must have one smart friend," she returned his tease. "But tell me, O cheerful one, what could be so bright about this place?"

"Well," said Leinad, pretending to think hard as he reached for another brick to hand to Tess. "We've got a lot more muscle to show for all of our work, while these overseers are getting fatter by the day. Why, look at you! You could take on any guy your age and pummel him to dust if you had a mind to."

The months of hard physical labor had indeed strengthened her form, and during the recent months, Tess's slender "little girl" body was slowly yielding to the developing form of a young girl in early adolescence.

Leinad had also changed. He had nearly lost his boyish look and had developed remarkable strength as well.

Tess gave Leinad a friendly push and changed her smirk

for the smile he had grown accustomed to. She took the brick from him and turned to place it. When she turned back, her smile vanished and concern clouded her face.

"Leinad, you should go for some water," she said rather earnestly.

"It is not time, Sunshine. What's the—"

He turned to see what had drawn her attention. Two guards were coming, on a target hunt for Fairos's courtyard duels. The work stopped, and the male slaves all tried to blend into the bricks.

"Please go, Leinad," she said desperately.

"If it's my time, I will not hide and let others suffer in my place. Don't worry, Sunshine. I can take care of myself," he said, trying to calm her down, but it did not seem to help.

The guards already had one victim and were looking for another. "You," one of the guards called to a middle-aged man just up the line from Leinad, "come with us."

The people turned to resume their work at the curses of the overseers. Tess breathed a sigh of relief.

"Today Lord Fairos wants a little extra challenge," the guard said with a smile and continued down the line.

The people stopped their work again, and Tess closed her eyes.

"Here's a young buck that ought to move fast enough to provide a little entertainment for Lord Fairos," the other guard said. They both stopped at Leinad, and he did not shrink back from them.

"Yes, we'll take him." One of the guards grabbed Leinad by the arm.

"No! Please, no!" Tess grabbed the guard's arm, and he recoiled with anger while the other drew his sword.

"Back off, girl!" the guard shouted.

"Tess!" Leinad said. "It will be all right."

He grabbed her hands and looked straight into her eyes. His firm confidence seemed to soothe her momentarily. He let go of her hands, and an overseer yelled for her to return to work. The guards escorted Leinad and the other two men to the courtyard.

Fairos was warming up with one of his guards. The clang of swords was a welcome sound to Leinad, for it reminded him of the days of training with his father in the meadow. Instinctively, he began to study Fairos as he fought. *He is weak to his left and his thrusts are shallow,* Leinad thought as his mind quickly adjusted from slave to sword fighter.

The courtyard was large and beautiful. Well-manicured bushes and hedges framed the lush, green grass. The training arena was large and rectangular with smooth, flat stones for a floor. Except for the perimeter posts, most of the guards were brought in to see the fight and to provide the cheers that Fairos loved to hear.

The captain of the guards placed the three men in one corner of the arena and put swords in their hands. Leinad glanced at the guard's side and recognized the beautiful hilt of his own sword. The slave trader must have sold it to him. Leinad vowed to one day recover the sword and free himself.

The captain stepped back to join the other guards, who were already laughing and joking in anticipation.

The middle-aged man was obviously very afraid. The sword he was holding might as well have been a fish. It was clear that he had never even held a sword before. The other man looked to be a couple of years older than Leinad and seemed slightly more comfortable with a sword. For Leinad, holding the sword was like shaking hands with an old friend. The hilt felt good, and though the balance of the sword was not right, it would do.

"I am Leinad," he said facing the other two. "What are your names?"

"My name is Quinn," the other young man said. His hair was sand-colored and complemented his handsome features. Leinad searched his eyes and saw fear but also courage.

"I am Osmar," the middle-aged man said.

"Have either of you ever trained with a sword before?" Leinad asked.

"Just a bit," Quinn said. "Never for blood, though, and not by anyone with experience."

Osmar looked at the ground. "Never. I was a farmer before here."

"It's okay, Osmar. We'll get you out of here alive, just stay behind me." Leinad looked at Quinn. "When he engages us, you move to his left, and I will take his right. Until I can blow the dust off my training, I need you to help keep him somewhat distracted. Okay?"

"I'll do what I can," said Quinn, trying to get a feel for his sword.

Leinad liked Quinn. He seemed to have a good heart.

Leinad gave them some basic points on defending themselves while Fairos finished his warm-up with the guard. Quinn seemed to at least follow Leinad's instruction, but Osmar responded only with a blank stare.

"Bring my enemies to me!" Fairos shouted just before quenching his thirst with a long, deep drink of water from a glass offered by a servant.

A couple of guards broke from the rest and guided Leinad, Quinn, and Osmar to the center of the arena near Fairos.

Fairos handed his glass to the servant and waved him off. He walked toward the men and slowly circled them, evaluating the potential skill of his next victims. He hardly glanced at Osmar, then hesitated behind Leinad and Quinn. He returned to the front and squinted at Leinad. He leaned forward and whispered in Leinad's ear.

"You hide your fear well, boy. But don't worry…in a few moments that will change." He stepped back and smiled condescendingly, but Leinad did not respond even with his eyes.

Fairos turned his back and walked away from them a few paces. "If you give me a good fight, I may not kill you. Do you understand?"

There was silence from the three men, and Fairos drew his sword. The two guards backed off with the others to watch. Leinad was first to position himself, and Quinn moved to his right side and raised his sword. Osmar was on Leinad's left. He lifted his sword and waited for Fairos to hit it. The fight was on.

Fairos laughed at Osmar and initiated a quick side cut on Osmar's blade and followed with a thrust to his chest. Leinad reached and deflected the thrust with his blade.

Fairos's sword passed just to the left of Osmar, and Leinad pushed him back and out of the way. Fairos showed surprise at the speed of Leinad's maneuver and repositioned to face him head-on. Leinad took the stance of a swordsman, and Fairos raised an eyebrow in apparent delight.

Quinn attempted a slice. Fairos parried and countered with a cut that nearly slit Quinn's throat. Leinad advanced with a simple combination to pull him off Quinn. Fairos now seemed to realize that Leinad was much more than a mere farm boy turned slave. He countered Leinad and advanced. He then quickly turned on Quinn. Quinn defended himself as best as he could, but Fairos was too strong and too experienced. Two quick engagements left Quinn open for a deadly thrust. As Fairos's blade advanced, Leinad again tried to deflect his sword, but he was too late. His attempt moved the blade off Quinn's heart, but that was all. The cold steel penetrated deep into Quinn's right shoulder.

Fairos quickly withdrew, and Quinn screamed in pain as he dropped his sword and fell to the ground, clutching his shoulder. Leinad moved to cover Quinn's position. Fairos backed off and lowered his sword.

Leinad knew Quinn's scream would carry beyond the courtyard and into the ears of the working slaves. It was a sound they heard often, each time followed by a brief intrusion of dread. He thought of Tess and wished he could spare her the anguish he knew she was experiencing.

"Remove the wounded, and put the other imbecile back on the wall," Fairos said as he pointed with his sword toward Osmar.

Two guards pulled Quinn to his feet. He looked at Leinad as if to apologize, but Leinad nodded his assurance and thanks. Leinad already knew more about Fairos than Fairos knew about him…the advantage was Leinad's. The guards guided Quinn to the edge of the arena, where two servants began bandaging his wound.

A young lad carrying a boy-size sword ran into the courtyard and over to Fairos. "Father! Father! Can I help you kill the slave?" he asked exuberantly.

Fairos knelt down and smiled at his son. "Watch closely, son. One day you will learn to fight like me and be the most powerful lord in the land."

"Yes, Father." The boy smiled and then sneered at Leinad.

"Where is you mother, Nevin?" Fairos asked.

"She's in the garden. She says she doesn't like to see all the blood."

Fairos smiled, "Yes, that is for men like us, Nevin. Now go stand with Captain Keston and watch."

The boy moved to the edge of the arena, swishing his sword back and forth at imaginary opponents. Fairos stood and turned toward Leinad.

"Let's get down to business, shall we, boy?"

His arrogance permeated the air. Leinad responded with a fight-ready stance.

Fairos immediately took the offensive and advanced with multiple combinations and thrusts. Leinad defended each stroke with focus and caution. His skill had not abandoned him, but his movements were no longer automatic, and he had to concentrate on each one. Slowly, Leinad's muscles began to remember their former training. With each parry and counter, he sloughed the persona of slave and donned the cloak of expert swordsman.

All the while, Leinad was studying Fairos. He was a formidable foe. He fought ruthlessly and aggressively. It was a style Leinad was not accustomed to. There were clearly no rules of engagement to which Fairos adhered, and thus Leinad fought with strength tempered by caution.

The castle guards were no longer jesting or talking. Silence gripped them as this duel of mastery unfolded. They moved closer to the fight and gawked in surprise over the skill this slave possessed.

"You fight well," Fairos said after Leinad thwarted yet another attack. "Where did you learn to fight?"

"I was taught by my father, sir."

Leinad took the opportunity to test an offensive combination. A cut, a slice, and a cut followed by a quick thrust nearly landed his blade in Fairos's shoulder, but a last-second parry deflected the blade just to the right of his arm. Leinad longed for the well-balanced strength of his own sword. In a duel of such closely matched skill, even the smallest hindrance could mean defeat.

Fairos laughed with delight. "You've been holding back, boy!"

Fairos began fighting with a new level of intensity and seemed to hold nothing back. Leinad now faced the full aggression of a battle-experienced warrior.

The guards and Quinn watched intently as the ferocious fight between boy and castle lord wore on.

Both men were breathing hard and sweating profusely.

The physical strain was tremendous for both of them, and Leinad was beginning to struggle. He was fighting for his life now, and though his training was exceptional, it was clear that he was not the equal of Lord Fairos.

Fairos brought advance after advance, putting Leinad in constant retreat. Leinad's sword flew to meet each cut, but his strength and will were faltering. Fairos seemed to sense victory approaching and pressed even harder. Leinad managed to counter with a cut and a reserved thrust, but Fairos parried the thrust and countered with a powerful slice. Leinad recovered just in time to meet the massive blow with his sword. The swords collided, and Leinad's sword snapped midway down the blade.

Fairos coiled back for the final blow. Leinad readied himself for death, but he did not cower. Filling his lungs with a final breath, he stood tall and looked Fairos square in the eyes. Fairos appeared surprised by the response. His sword was raised and ready to strike, but it did not move.

Quinn turned away, not wanting to witness the death of his newfound companion.

"Kill him, Father! Kill him!" Leinad heard Fairos's son yell from the side of the arena.

The sun gleamed off the raised blade of the bloodthirsty warrior, but Fairos's countenance changed and he lowered his sword.

"Relax, boy. You will live another day," he said to Leinad, less condescending than a short time ago. "All of my guards have faced the steel of my sword early in their service to me. They fear me, boy. Do you?"

Fairos did not wait for an answer but turned to face his

castle guards and called to them. "Who among you will fight this boy to the death?"

Fairos's only response from the men was silence and down-turned eyes.

"That's what I thought," Fairos said. "That is why… what's your name, boy?"

"I am Leinad."

"That is why Leinad will become your trainer. I do not have the time to train you effectively, and the boy is obviously capable. For training exercises, you will do exactly as he says." Fairos glared at his men. "Do you understand me?"

"Yes, Lord Fairos," came their unanimous reply.

"Leinad, tomorrow you will begin training my guards. The captain of the guards will schedule individual training with each one. You are still a slave here, but if you serve me well, that can change." Fairos stared hard into Leinad's eyes. "Kneel and swear your allegiance to me so that I know there will be no treachery from you within my castle."

The voice of his father whispered in Leinad's heart. "I cannot swear my allegiance to you, sir, for it belongs to one man only…the King of Arrethtrae. But I swear by the honor of my father that I will train your men without deceit, as you desire."

Fairos's eyes narrowed. "As far as you are concerned, boy, I am your king."

Leinad's resolve was evident, but Fairos clearly did not want to lose an opportunity to improve the effectiveness of his force by unnecessarily killing the talented youth.

"But for now, I will accept your word." Fairos called for his servants. "Take the boy, feed him, and clean him up."

"Sir," Leinad said, "there is one request I would humbly ask of you to improve the effectiveness of the training."

Fairos stared at Leinad. "What is it?"

"The captain of your guards took possession of my sword when I became a slave here. I humbly ask for it to be returned so that I may carry out your wishes to my utmost." Leinad wondered if he'd crossed the line.

Fairos hesitated and then turned to the captain of the guards. "Keston, return the sword. When you can best him, it is yours again."

Fairos left the courtyard with his son under his arm.

As Keston reluctantly handed the magnificent sword over, the sneer on his face made it quite clear to Leinad the depth of bitterness this humiliation caused the man. Leinad had just made an enemy, and he made a mental note never to turn his back on Keston.

Leinad was pleased to resume training with his own sword, but his spirit was also troubled. By his expertise, Fairos's power and influence would grow. *Should I have accepted death to prevent Fairos's expansion? What will my fellow slaves think of me? What will become of Tess now that I am not there to protect her? What would the King of Arrethtrae want…the King that I have never seen?*

This turn of events was completely unexpected, and Leinad felt uneasy with his new position. It was a path he never anticipated. It was a path he felt ill-prepared to take.

## CHAPTER ELEVEN

# A SAVAGE BATTLE

Living conditions for Leinad improved greatly once he became Fairos's trainer. All of the amenities of the castle were his, though his conscience prohibited him from indulging beyond his needs. He was even allowed a certain amount of freedom as Fairos's trust in him grew. However, his heart was ever upon the slaves beyond the castle's inner walls. He was able to get Tess assigned to lighter duty, but it was small compensation for the hardship he knew she was enduring. He asked Quinn to watch out for her when he could not. Although he was bound by his word, the thought of true and complete freedom was always on his mind. Even though he might find a way to escape, he knew he could never leave without Tess.

Leinad trained Fairos's men daily, imitating the training his father had given him. The guards improved dramatically and were quickly becoming a skilled and disciplined force. Fairos told Leinad that he was pleased with the transformation.

"My power in Nyland and in the kingdom is growing," he said to Leinad in an unguarded moment. "I will be the most powerful man in the land!"

One day, Leinad's training was interrupted by an alarm from the guard stationed on the southeast watchtower. "Rider approaching!"

There was urgency in the rider's approach, and Keston halted the training sessions and reported this news to Fairos. Fairos entered the courtyard just as the rider charged through the gate.

He jumped from his horse and quickly knelt before Fairos. "My Lord Fairos, have mercy."

"Rise and speak," Fairos commanded.

The man stood and drew a deep breath. "I was sent by the people of the Valley of Nan. We received word that the Eminafs were approaching our valley. With almost no defenses, our only hope was to leave the valley and find protection, so we set out for Nyland two days ago. The Eminafs have discovered us, and their entire force is nearly upon us. Please, Lord Fairos, help us! They are a vicious people, and no one will survive if you do not help."

"Who are the Eminafs?" Leinad asked.

Fairos turned toward Leinad, and concern was on his face. "They are bloodthirsty nomadic warriors. They travel from region to region, killing and stealing everything they find. In times past we have suffered the edge of their swords as well." He paused for a moment, then turned back to the messenger.

"How many of your people are there?" he asked.

"Two hundred, maybe."

Leinad knew that Fairos would never take a risk without the possibility of gaining more in return. Regardless of the motives of Fairos, he knew that he needed to help save the people of Nan.

"I called the Valley of Nan home once, Lord Fairos," Leinad said. "These people helped me. Please let me go and help them."

Leinad could see that Fairos was intensely focused as he considered the situation. It was at times like this that Leinad understood why Fairos was the powerful man he was. He began to speak his thoughts.

"Once the Eminafs are finished with the people of Nan, Nyland and my castle will become their next target." Fairos paused. "I will not wait and let them lay siege to my castle or destroy my land. Most of the Eminafs will not be mounted, but we will be, so we will attack them on the plains in the open. Though they may outnumber us, we will have the advantage." He turned to Leinad. "With the skills you have honed in my men, we will destroy the Eminafs once and for all! Keston, prepare the men—we leave immediately!"

All but a handful of guards were soon mounted and exiting the castle across the drawbridge. Leinad found the familiar eyes of his friend and read the concern in her countenance. All he could do to reassure Tess was to nod and wink. Quinn stood beside her and returned Leinad's farewell with a casual salute.

Fairos's army rode east toward the Valley of Nan. Most of the men wore helmets and armor. Leinad wore a leather tunic and carried only his sword. He had tried the armor once, but did not like how it slowed his movements and restricted his vision.

"How far out are your people?" Fairos shouted to the messenger above the sound of galloping horses.

"No more than an hour's ride, my lord."

As Fairos's force of nearly two hundred men crested a hill, Leinad felt anxiety in his stomach. A battle scene was unfolding before them. The people of Nan were a short distance from the base of the hill that Fairos's forces were descending. The vicious Eminafs were nearly upon them, and their savage cry filled the air. Those that were mounted led the barbaric army, but once they saw Fairos's men, they fell back with the rest of their ground warriors before resuming their advance. Leinad estimated that the Eminafs outnumbered them two to one.

"To battle!" Fairos yelled as he led the charge down the hill toward the advancing Eminafs.

His men shouted in unison and drew their swords. Never having experienced a real battle, Leinad wanted to stay close to Fairos and learn quickly how to fight and survive.

The people of Nan were sandwiched between two forces, each screaming and charging with weapons before them. They continued their flight toward Fairos and up the hill.

Fairos ordered his men to split into a left and right flank to allow the people of Nan passage through their charge. The division put them at an immediate advantage by allowing them to engage the Eminafs on two fronts. Leinad and half of the men followed Fairos to the right, while Keston led the other half to the left.

Just moments before the Eminafs would have crushed

the people of Nan, Fairos and his men engaged the blood-thirsty warriors with full force. The distinct line of forces quickly dissolved into a wild mesh of crashing steel and armor.

Leinad thought the mere sight of the Eminafs up close was enough to unsettle even the bravest of men. Their faces were painted to appear as skeletons. Wild hair flowed from their heads in an unnatural orange-brown color. Almost none of them wore armor, and their swords were sinister, with extra short blades protruding from the handle guards. What Leinad found most unsettling, though, was their shrill battle cry.

The mounted Eminafs were the first to engage and the first to fall. The advantage of Fairos's mounted men over the Eminafs' ground forces was significant indeed, and the numbers soon became equal. The Eminafs turned to attacking the horses of Fairos's men to equalize their fighting position. Leinad's own steed was taken out as well, and he found himself on foot in the midst of the deadly battle.

Leinad focused on each encounter while maintaining awareness outside his own arena. The recent months of fine-tuning his skills rewarded him. Sword fight after sword fight, his blade flew to vanquish these warriors of terror.

Fairos's men fought superbly because of the training Leinad had given them. As the battle wore on, the Eminafs began to falter and attempted a retreat, but Fairos pursued them with his men that were still mounted and gave no mercy. Their casualties were minimal compared to the decimation of the Eminafs. The battle belonged completely to Fairos.

Upon his return, the men cheered Fairos in their triumph. He sought Leinad out and praised him for the excellent training he had given the men. Leinad was thankful to have saved his people, but the bitter taste of battle was hard to swallow.

Fairos and his men escorted the people of Nan through Nyland and on toward the castle. Fairos allowed them to camp a short distance from the castle and even provided food and fresh water, but Leinad became concerned, for he knew the heart of Fairos. Leinad visited the people in their camp and talked to their leaders.

"You must leave this land at once!" he told them.

"The people are weary, and we have nowhere to go," one of the men said. "This is good land. Here is where we will make our home."

"You don't understand! Once Fairos is organized and ready, he will make slaves of you all. Then you will never be able to leave!"

Just as Leinad finished speaking, Fairos and fifty of his men rode into camp. His face of compassion was gone. He approached the circle of men and remained on his horse.

"Leinad, wandering a bit far from the castle, aren't we?" he said with a patronizing tone. "I wonder what brings you out here today?"

He spoke harshly to the men standing before Leinad. "Gather your people so they can hear me."

Within a few moments, the people of Nan were gathered together, and Fairos's men quietly encircled them.

"Fairos, please don't do this," Leinad said as he saw the inevitable unfold. Fairos ignored him.

"People of Nan, I hope your stay here has been a pleasant one," he shouted for all to hear. "Because from this moment forward, you will be my slaves."

The people's voices rose in alarm and petition. Fairos gave his men a signal, and they all drew their swords. The people hushed to silence.

"You have no place to go and no food to eat. I will give you both, and in exchange you will work for me. Work hard and you will live. Work sluggishly and you will be punished. Try to escape and you will die! Do you understand?"

Once again the people murmured angrily in protest, but the guards closed in on them. Leinad felt anger mounting within him.

"Fairos, you cannot do this to these people," Leinad exclaimed. "They came to you helpless, and now you turn them into slaves? What kind of a man are you?"

Fairos glared down at Leinad. "I am a man of great power, Leinad, and you are forgetting who you are!" Fairos's anger eased slightly. "Return to the castle before you do something we will both regret."

Leinad did not restrain his own anger. "If you enslave these people, I will no longer train your men!"

"What a shame, Leinad," Fairos said with contempt. "You could have been one of my best, but instead you will be a slave once more, and your people will suffer for your insolence." He turned to Keston. "Remove his sword, put him in peasant clothes, and take him to the wall. Tell the overseers to watch him closely. No longer will any of my men speak the name of Leinad. His name is *slave!*"

"Yes, my lord…gladly!" Keston smiled vengefully as he dismounted and removed the coveted sword. He ordered two guards to strip him. Keston escorted Leinad to the overseers and found numerous opportunities to strike him along the way.

"Mark my words, slave," Keston said as he struck Leinad across the back with the pommel of Leinad's sword. "Now that I have recovered my sword, a day is coming when I will recover my honor as well by killing you!"

## CHAPTER TWELVE

# JOURNEY TO DEATH

 Many months passed, and the yoke of slavery was heavy for the people. Some wondered if death would be their only escape from the torment. Lord Fairos's men increased their use of the whip to attain the level of productivity they desired. No one was exempt from punishment—not the old, not the sick, not the children.

The heat was stifling, the air heavy, damp, and still. In spite of the oppression, Leinad and Tess usually mustered the energy to pass an encouraging word to everyone they encountered during their labor.

"Leinad," Tess said softly one day, "our people are dying. Is there no one who cares? Is there no one who can deliver us from this bondage? I try to encourage the people, but it seems hopeless."

Tess's words were hard for Leinad to hear, for he was a young man dealing with intense guilt. His skill with the sword had saved the people, but it was also what had delivered them into bondage—a bondage that appeared to have no end. It was his sense of responsibility for Tess and for the people that kept him going.

"I will find a way out of—"

"Move it!" an overseer shouted to an old man as he struggled to carry a brick up a slight incline to the wall.

Leinad and Tess turned to see what poor soul was to be the focus of the abuse that was sure to come. The old man tried to quicken his pace, but he stumbled and fell. The overseer uncoiled his whip and struck the browned bare back. The old man moaned in pain and tried to recover, but the overseer cursed and laid another lash into the bleeding flesh.

Leinad's guilt quickly transformed into anger—anger that rivaled what he felt when the Dark Knight killed his father. Leinad ran to the old man and arrived just in time to thwart another whiplash. He now stood between the old man and his aggressor.

"Leave him be!" Leinad spoke with the courage of a man.

"As you wish, slave," came the sarcastic reply of the overseer. He pulled his whip back and released a lash on Leinad with all his might.

The whip struck Leinad's left shoulder, and it fully encircled him until the leather tip sliced into his back. Leinad wrapped his left arm around the whip and yanked the overseer toward him. As the unsuspecting overseer fell forward, Leinad landed a full-force fist into his jaw. The overseer fell to the ground unconscious, and the skirmish brought the attention of three other overseers in an instant. They forced Leinad into the dirt face-first and called for Barak, the head overseer.

"So, we have a feisty one I see," Barak said with a hint of pleasure in his voice. "Call for Lord Fairos," he commanded.

Barak was a large man with equal amounts of fat and muscle on his body. He was the most vicious of all the overseers. He knelt down, wedged his knee into the open wound on Leinad's back, and wrapped his whip around his neck. He pulled upward until Leinad was gasping for each breath.

Barak lowered his voice and spoke near to Leinad's ear. "You have forgotten that you are a mere slave now. We will use you to show the rest of these knaves what a little insolence will buy them."

Fairos arrived on the scene, already visibly angry from the messenger's report. "What is going on here!" he demanded.

By now most of the work had stopped on this side of the castle, and the people were easing close enough to hear and see what was happening.

"It seems we have a rebel in our midst," Barak said, and at last he released his noose from Leinad's neck.

Leinad gasped for air but felt as though his throat had collapsed permanently. By now the unconscious overseer was stirring.

"Get up!" Fairos said to the overseer. "You should be ashamed to be so easily humiliated by a slave. How could you have let that happen?"

"He...he attacked me from behind and hit me with a rock."

From the ground, Leinad saw the terrified face of Tess among the bystanders. He could tell she wanted to do something, but he shook his head slightly to restrain her from any foolish attempts at aid.

Fairos motioned for his men to lift Leinad to his feet. The dirt clung to his chest and face, and he still found it difficult to swallow, but at least he was able to fill his lungs.

"Why...it's the slave!" Fairos scoffed when he recognized Leinad. "Your rebellious acts are more than a nuisance to me, slave. For striking an overseer, the penalty is death." Fairos shook his head and ran his fingers through his hair. "However, I am not a man without principles. To kill one who helped me expand my power would be barbaric, and yet you are far too dangerous to let live."

Fairos looked over his land and into the faces of the people he had enslaved. "Tie him to the gates and whip him, but give him only ten lashes," he said to Barak. "Then you will take him to the desert and stake him down. We will let the Moshi Beast finish him off."

Fairos looked at Leinad with sadness and contempt. "I will not kill you, slave, but you will wish I had."

Barak smiled a devilish grin as he nodded a salute to Fairos. Barak ordered two overseers to take Leinad to the gate and bind him. The other overseers were told to gather the people. Barak cracked his whip in anticipation of his pleasure.

As he was being led away, Leinad saw Quinn work his way to Tess's side and place a consoling hand on her shoulder. She turned to Leinad, and the pain he saw in her face pierced his heart.

The overseers herded the people toward the castle gate, where Leinad was tied with both arms outstretched to the large posts on each side. Barak was anxiously cracking his whip and taunting his victim. Though he tried to control it,

Leinad could not subdue the fear welling up inside him. He knew that Barak's lashes would not sting like the one he had already received. They would tear. Barak would make sure of it.

When all the people were in place, Fairos spoke: "This slave struck one of my men and demonstrated a rebellious attitude, which will be punished. Do not make the same mistake, or you too will pay with your life!"

Fairos nodded, and Barak's whip split the air with a thunderous crack that penetrated deep into Leinad's skin. The pain was excruciating, but Leinad clenched his teeth and did not reward Barak with a scream. Another one followed—and another—and another. Each lash brought such intense pain that Leinad's body convulsed in spasms. With his arms outstretched, Leinad's gashes separated even further, adding to the unbearable pain. Barak sadistically reveled in the torture he was administering.

The women in the crowd turned away, and the children cried. The men watched silently, their faces reflecting both anger and fear.

*Father, where is the vision now?* Leinad screamed in his mind. *Our homes have been burned, our lands ravaged, our families enslaved. What hope is there? Where is our King who demands justice? Are we destined to die as slaves?*

Leinad's pain was deeper than even the wounds on his back.

The torment continued...five...six...seven lashes. Leinad now hung limp from the ropes that held him. Eight... Leinad could contain his pain no longer, and a muffled scream came from his mouth.

He looked into the crowd and saw Tess bury her head into Quinn's chest. She covered her ears to block the sound of the persecution. She had endured much throughout her life, but this seemed too much to bear.

Barak finished the final lashes, smiling with each moan he heard. The ropes were loosened. Leinad collapsed to his knees, and then to his hands.

Tess ran to him and fell to her knees beside him.

"Leinad," she half-whispered. Tears spilled from her eyes.

Leinad tilted his head her way. "Don't lose hope, Sunshine," he said with difficulty, for he had.

"Get away, girl!" one of the overseers yelled. He grabbed her arm and pushed her back into the crowd.

"Learn from what you have seen," Fairos said. "If you resist me or my men, you will be punished. Now get back to work!" He pompously turned and strode back to his castle.

With the prodding of the overseers and the castle guards, the solemn crowd moved back toward their work.

"Bind him and throw him into a brick cart," Keston ordered.

Barak and another overseer loaded the horse-drawn cart with its battered cargo and left Fairos's estate for the Banteen Desert. Leinad caught a glimpse of Tess falling to her knees and sobbing just before the cart rounded a grove of trees and Fairos's estate vanished from view.

Leinad was an unwilling passenger on a journey to death…a death that was to come at the jaws of the Moshi Beast.

## CHAPTER THIRTEEN

# STORM OF SALVATION

The journey into the Banteen Desert lasted for hours. The pain from the wounds on Leinad's back was almost more than he could bear. With each passing mile, the lush green landscape slowly gave way to dry, rocky desert.

They continued into the desert some distance before stopping. Barak and his man pounded four stakes into the sand. They stretched Leinad's arms and legs to tie them to the stakes, and he nearly passed out from the pain of reopening the gashes across his back. Leinad was faceup, his wounds pressed into the hot sand.

"Hurry it up, man," Barak said.

The other overseer was nervously looking at the desert horizon. "What dose this Moshi Beast look like?" he asked with apprehension in his voice.

"I don't know. I just know that the last slave we left here started screamin' not long after we left him, and I didn't wait around to see why. Later, I came back, and the only thing left was his bones."

The man's eyes widened, and he quickly finished tying Leinad's leg down.

Barak checked that each leather strap was secure and leaned close to Leinad's face. Beads of sweat mixed with the dirt on his fat face to form dark streaks that ran down his neck. He smiled an evil smile, revealing black frames around each ragged tooth. The stench in his breath was enough to make Leinad cough.

"I wish I could kill you myself, slave, but knowing the torment you'll feel is satisfaction enough."

He stood and kicked Leinad in the side. The pain churned Leinad's stomach, and he waited for it to subside, but it lingered long.

There were only a few more hours of daylight, and Leinad could not deny the fear and isolation that enveloped him as he saw Fairos's men mount their cart and return to the lush lands of the castle.

As they disappeared over the horizon, Leinad knew that he was facing his final few hours—maybe his final few moments. He pulled hard on the ties that bound him, but they were secure. After hours of pulling on his bindings, his only reward was a small crack in the soil surrounding each stake. He lay exhausted, trying to imagine what the Moshi Beast looked like. He wondered how long it would take for it to find him.

The end of the day approached and night fell. Leinad slept a few fitful moments, but his muscles ached from inactivity, and the chill night air made him miserable.

By the next afternoon, the sun was blistering hot, and there was still no sign of the Moshi Beast. Leinad's lips began to dry and crack. He thought he might die from the heat of the sun rather than by the teeth of the Moshi Beast.

As the hours passed, his fear subsided some, and he became weary of searching his surroundings for this dreaded creature. Leinad spotted two vultures circling high above him. The sun was still blistering hot, but a few clouds invaded the blue sky to give him occasional relief from the direct sunlight.

Off to his left he spotted movement, and his fear immediately returned. Leinad was relieved when he saw a small animal with brown fur emerge from behind a desert bush. It was the size of a large squirrel, but its tail was short. Black stripes zigzagged up and down from the front of its body to its tail on both sides. Its ears were large for the size of its head. The animal timidly made its way to Leinad and stood upon its hind legs to get a better view of this strange sight.

"Hello, little guy," Leinad said gently so as not to frighten him.

The little critter twitched its nose to smell him.

"You haven't seen a mean ol' Moshi Beast around here, have you?" he asked, thankful for the company even if it was a rodent.

The little critter chirped as if to respond to Leinad's question. It moved closer to Leinad's left side, under his out-stretched arm.

"No, I didn't think so. Well, I hope the Beast doesn't like furry little brown critters…for your sake." He smiled at his new little friend. Leinad could feel the moist nose of the critter as it sniffed him some more.

"If I were you—ouch!" Leinad yelled.

The critter chirped excitedly and ran a few paces away.

"You bit me!" Leinad was bleeding from a pea-sized tear in his flesh.

The critter turned and ran off, chirping continuously.

"Some friend you are!" He wanted to coddle the new wound but was helpless to do so. Leinad could not remember ever being more miserable. The clouds in the sky above thickened to accompany his despair.

Moments later, he heard a faint, high-pitched sound. It grew louder with each passing second until Leinad recognized its source, and pure dread filled his heart. The sound of thousands of individual chirps grew steadily until he could hear no other sound.

© Marcella Johnson

The bright blue sky was completely gone now, obliterated by thick, dark clouds, and so was any fringe of hope Leinad ever had of living. The leading edge of a mass of brown chirping critters flowed toward Leinad like a wave rushing toward the waiting shoreline, anxious to crash upon its banks. The chirping was deafening.

The Moshi Beasts encircled Leinad. He yelled at them, and the beasts in front retreated slightly, but only temporarily. Leinad strained at the leather straps and stakes in near panic as he yelled again, but this time the Moshi Beasts did not yield in their approach.

He felt a small piece of flesh torn from his right thigh...then his left. He screamed as dozens of carnivorous teeth sank into his body at once.

All of a sudden, the sky exploded with sound as a lightning bolt ripped through the air, sending its thunder in all directions. The Moshi Beasts scurried for cover beneath bushes and rocks.

Leinad was thankful for the temporary reprieve, but he wondered how long it would last. He bled from two dozen bites all over his body. The thunder had silenced the Moshi Beasts, and the momentary silence was a relief.

A moment passed, and Leinad heard the first chirp, quickly followed by many more. As the Moshi Beasts regained their confidence, they once more surrounded Leinad.

*Please...no...not again! My King...will You let me die this lonely death?*

The beasts closed in again, slowly returning to their feast, but a few large raindrops pounded the dusty soil beside them and they hesitated.

*Crack!* Another lightning bolt exploded just a few hundred paces away, and the rain increased in intensity. It was too much for the Moshi Beasts, and they scurried back en masse in the direction they had come from.

The rain now began to fall in sheets and soaked Leinad in an instant. The water ran down his body and into the

sores, painfully washing each one. He knew that the Moshi Beasts would return as soon as the storm passed. He opened his mouth to catch as much water to drink as possible. The cool, refreshing wash rejuvenated him, both inside and out. The provisional peace was enough, and he lay still, enjoying his final moments of respite.

When he had drunk enough, he slowly turned his head and looked at the stake holding his right arm. He saw a tiny rivulet of water flowing into the crack near its base, which had been formed by his earlier attempts to pull free. A sliver of hope softly landed in his mind.

He concentrated on that one stake. First he pulled toward him—then up—then down. With each movement, the soil loosened, and the crack grew bigger—and so did the river that flowed into it. He worked fervently to loosen the stake. But his arm grew fatigued, and he was forced to rest.

Leinad stopped only long enough to allow his arm time to recuperate. The crack was now the size of his finger...then his thumb. He strained at the stake to move it upward, but it did not give.

The rain lightened.

Again he pulled and widened the stake hole even more. He tried to lift the stake once more, and it moved! Leinad paused and garnered the strength for one last pull. He grunted and lifted with all his strength.

At last, the stake pulled free.

Leinad was expressly aware that the rain had stopped, and the clouds were beginning to dissipate. It took a monumental effort to reach for the strap that held his other arm. His muscles were stiff, and the sores on his back and sides resisted all movement. He loosened the strap and freed his arm, then worked on the straps that held his legs. Soon he was free and made an attempt to stand. He became dizzy and nearly fainted, but steadied himself until the blood returned to his head.

As the sun peeked from behind the remaining storm clouds, Leinad heard the familiar terrorizing sound of the Moshi Beasts. They were returning!

Leinad forced himself to move in the opposite direction. With each step, strength returned to his legs, and he remembered how to run. He moved as fast as he could, but the sound of the Moshi Beasts grew steadily in spite of his efforts. His lungs began to hurt, but he pressed on.

The ground rose slightly ahead of him, and he could not see beyond the crest of the nearby horizon. The brown mass of chirping Moshi Beasts was closing on him quickly. He reached the top of the rise and saw a large earth basin not more that a hundred paces away. The surrounding terrain fed water into the basin to form a temporary oasis whenever it rained. A large tree grew at the far end of the shallow pond.

Leinad knew he would not make the tree in time. He figured that the Moshi Beasts might be able to climb anyway, so he sprinted for the shallow pond.

He looked behind him, and the beasts were almost upon him. The last few paces seemed agonizingly long, but he dove for the water just as the Moshi Beasts reached his feet. He splashed wildly, expecting to feel the searing bites all over his body once again—but he did not.

Leinad stood in knee-deep water and looked at the edge of the pond just a few steps away. The Moshi Beasts were gathered and chirping at the edge, but they did not advance past the waterline. Their incessant chirping seemed to scold Leinad for ruining their feast.

He fell to his knees, exhausted and sore…but saved.

The Moshi Beasts eventually left to search for other prey, but Leinad stayed in the water many hours beyond their departure. He quenched his thirst with the murky water, but his hunger grew. Weariness pulled at his limbs, and he made his way to the far end of the pond where the tree stood.

Leinad was exhausted, having gone two days with no sleep and no food. He was in pain, having endured the lashes of Barak, the scorch of the sun, and the bites of the Moshi Beasts. He did not dare leave the water, but he could not lie down and sleep either.

He fell to his hands and knees at the water's edge, beneath the shade of the large tree. He crawled to the base of the tree and laid his head in the mud, just out of the water.

Other animals came to drink from the water, which would not last long, but Leinad did not notice. He was deep in the cavern of sleep.

## CHAPTER FOURTEEN

# A QUESTION
# OF FAITH

 When Leinad awoke, it was dark, and he was cold. He did not know how long he had slept, but the cool night air indicated that morning was close. The water had receded beyond where his feet lay. Leinad was thankful the Moshi Beasts had not returned, for his protection would soon be gone. He knew the desert drank up any standing water within days of a heavy rainstorm.

At first, his arms and legs refused to move. He forced himself to crawl the remaining distance to the base of the tree and leaned against its trunk. He pulled his knees close to his chest to retain what body heat was left. Dried mud clung to his skin from his face to his feet.

He shivered and looked up into the branches of the tree and was strangely comforted. His mind was drawn back to another tree years ago that had shaded him and his father back on the Plains of Kerr near their farm. He ached for those pleasant times and the companionship of his father.

The dawn was edging closer to begin another day, and first light began to break the night-sky blackness.

"Father, did you know what would become of your son?" he asked out loud, breaking the desert night silence. "Did you know that your training would lead me to this desolate place?"

Leinad began to question all that he was taught. Questions rose that he had not dared to ask before, but the solitude of the desert night forced them from his lips.

"Who is this King that you taught me to serve? Who is this King that you taught me to honor? Who is this King that you say loves this land and the people in it?"

Only silence replied, and he wondered if he would ever know.

"I AM!" A powerful voice shattered both the silence and his questions.

Leinad leapt to his feet and turned. The rush in his body overcame any pain he was feeling. Not sure of where the voice came from, he crouched and searched in fear.

"Who's there?"

"Leinad…do not be afraid," the rich voice responded compassionately.

"Who are You?"

Leinad realized that the voice came from the other side of the tree, and he moved to the side to see better. The morning light was growing. A majestic form adorned in royal clothes stood before him. A white stallion stood beside the figure.

Leinad thought he must still be dreaming, or perhaps hallucinating from lack of food. He trembled not only because of the chill of the night, but also because of the power that emanated from the one before him.

"Who are You, sir?" he repeated.

The one before him did not seem to need the morning light. His stature was regal, and the likeness of His face was majestic. Though His eyes seemed to burn like fire, compassion accompanied His gaze.

"Leinad—"

He had never heard his name spoken with such depth of familiarity.

"I am the One your father taught you to serve. I am the One he taught you to honor. I am the One who loves this land and the people in it. I am your King!"

His words resonated off the basin slopes, and Leinad felt more insignificant in His presence than he had ever felt before. Now he trembled in his heart for having doubted the one who stood before him. He knelt before the King in humility.

"Please forgive me, my King. I am not worthy to be in Your presence."

The King walked toward Leinad and stood before him. "Rise, Leinad."

Leinad slowly stood but dared not look the King full in the face.

"You have been faithful, but yet you doubted," the King said. "Now be faithful...and never doubt."

Leinad slowly looked up and beheld the royal King.

"I shall never doubt again, my Lord."

The King penetrated Leinad's thoughts with His eyes.

There was nothing Leinad could hide from the King, and he knew it. The King smiled and placed His hand on Leinad's shoulder.

"Come, Leinad. You must eat and heal."

The King gave Leinad food and fresh water that nourished his body and his spirit. He also gave Leinad water to wash off the mud and to clean himself. The King dressed Leinad's wounds with the same sweet smelling ointment Gabrik had used on Peyton, and then He covered them with bandages. He gave Leinad fresh clothes that fit him perfectly.

Leinad had shoes on his feet, clothes on his body, and food in his stomach. By late afternoon, Leinad felt human once again, but he was still exhausted from the previous day's ordeal.

"Lie down and rest, Leinad," the King said.

"But my Lord, what if the Moshi Beasts return?"

The King looked at Leinad unconcerned. "They will not return. Rest."

Leinad submitted and lay down beneath the large shade tree. The sun did not seem as hot, and his wounds did not seem to hurt as much. Within moments, he fell into a long, sweet, peaceful sleep.

When he awoke, the crisp desert morning air greeted him, and so did the smell of breakfast cooking on a fire. Leinad had slept the rest of the day and on through the night. The King gave Leinad food to eat but took none for Himself.

Midway through breakfast, Leinad realized in astonishment that the wounds on his body did not hurt. He gingerly felt under his arm where the first Moshi Beast had bitten him.

"You may remove the bandages at your convenience," the King said. "Your wounds are healed."

Leinad pressed where the wound ought to be and felt nothing. He looked at the King in amazement. "But—"

"Leinad, from this day forward, you will no longer question the purpose of your mission." The King spoke firmly and with incredible authority.

Leinad was still amazed at the release of pain, but the King's words enticed him to listen closely.

"The people I have chosen are in bondage under Fairos of Nyland. I have heard their cries, and the time for their deliverance is now." He paused. "You will deliver them."

Leinad's eyes widened. "But my King, I am but one man, and Fairos is powerful and an experienced warrior. How could I possibly free the people?"

"I will be your power, and I will give you the experience you need to defeat him."

Leinad slowly shook his head. "Surely, my King, You must seek someone better than me…some mighty warrior with an army of gallant men. I could not possibly do what You—"

"Leinad!" The King's voice was quite forceful. "I have chosen you for this day. I know you better than you know yourself. I will prepare you for this crusade."

Leinad bowed low. "Yes, my King. I will try with my very life to do as You ask."

The King went to the white stallion and retrieved an object wrapped in fine linen.

"Are you ready to accept the responsibility of one who serves the King?" he asked Leinad.

"I am, my Lord."

"Then take your sword and boldly follow Me!" commanded the King as He unveiled Leinad's sword.

"My sword!"

"I gave this sword to you years ago because through it I will deliver My people." The King allowed Leinad to take the sword. "You were chosen to carry the sword because your heart was always loyal and true to Me. You may not have understood the significance then, but today begins your transformation…and the kingdom's transformation through its might. I will help you unlock the power of this sword to do My will and begin to transform this kingdom from chaos to hope."

Leinad held the sword and looked upon its beauty with a new understanding. The mark of the King in the pommel was prominent. In his awe, Leinad realized that it had never been *his* sword. It was, and always would be, the King's.

"I thought Keston had the sword. How did You get it?" Leinad asked.

"No one carries a sword that bears My mark except by My permission. Are you fit for training, young Leinad?"

"Yes, my King!"

Leinad remembered that his father had told him how the King Himself trained him. Now it was Leinad's time. The thought of being trained by the greatest swordsman in all of Arrethtrae and beyond, and being reunited with the sword, invigorated Leinad.

"What your father began, I shall complete."

The King unsheathed a sword that had no equal...nor ever would. It seemed to glow in its magnificence, and Leinad stared in awe at its glory. So this was the sword that Gabrik and his father had talked of that day in Mankin—the King's sword! Leinad felt honored and humbled at the same time. Who was he to have this honor bestowed on him? He relished the moment and was determined to learn as much as possible from the majestic King and His sword.

The training was difficult and demanding. The King seemed tireless. Each night Leinad fell to sleep exhausted and awoke to delicious provisions and a refreshed body. The King was always there...waiting patiently for the dawn to arrive...looking beyond the horizon to the future of His kingdom and His people.

Through the days and weeks that followed, the King brought Leinad's skill with the sword to a level of mastery never attained by any man born this side of the Great Sea. Finally the day came when Leinad's training was complete.

The following morning when Leinad awoke, the King was not nearby as He usually was. After some searching, Leinad spotted His regal form standing atop the basin hill, against the bluish-pink skyline. Leinad cautiously approached Him from behind, not wishing to disturb Him as He gazed into the distant lands of the kingdom. Though Leinad's approach was nearly silent, there was no surprise in the King.

"Leinad," the King said, "with what I have given you, there is only one who can defeat you now."

"The Dark Knight, my Lord?"

"No. The one I speak of is more dangerous than even

he...it is you yourself, Leinad." The King turned and looked at Leinad with those eyes that burned like fire.

Leinad was taken aback and did not understand.

"If you begin to rely upon yourself and become arrogant in your skill, that is the day you will fall." The King's gaze was hard and serious. "You must always come back to Me, Leinad. Never forget who you serve."

Leinad knelt before the King.

"My sword is Yours, my hands and arms are Yours, my heart is Yours, and my life is Yours. I shall always be humble before You and before my fellow servants. On Your sword I swear it."

The King drew His sword from His scabbard one last time. "You knelt as Leinad of Kerr and of Nan, but you will rise as Sir Leinad, Knight of the King!"

The King knighted Leinad in the harsh landscape of the desert, the only place where a man truly begins to understand his purpose in life. Leinad was a man in his own right, but he was a knight by the King's right. Although the future was not clear, the vision he'd been searching for was. For the first time in his life, Leinad did not question who he was or where he was going. Nor did he doubt the King he served. His path was set, his heart firm, and his mind secure.

Leinad journeyed to call his people to freedom, and the blades of one thousand warriors would not stop him. For as the King said it, so shall it be.

# AT KINGDOM'S EDGE

 Leinad's story is not over, but I am afraid I cannot tell its end just now. My own journey awaits me, Cedric of Chessington, and I must pause the tale to resume my own course.

The ship's crew is rising to their duties, and I can hear the anxious pawing and neighing of our mounts beneath the deck. They desire to feel the solid ground under their hooves again, for it has been a long journey. They need not wait long now. I can see a jagged break in the smooth, watery horizon. The shores of Arrethtrae await our arrival.

Ah, the knights on the flagship ahead are preparing to disembark. I hope you will join me again soon, for the saga of gallant Sir Leinad is the foundation of my own life and very possibly yours as well.

It is a story worth its telling indeed!

# DISCUSSION QUESTIONS

To further facilitate the understanding of the biblical allegory of this series, a few discussion questions and answers are provided below.

CHAPTER 1

1. Peyton represents Adam, and Leinad represents the Old Testament prophets and devout men of God from Seth to Malachi. What does the sword represent, and why does Leinad question the training his father is giving him?

2. The Great Sea separates the kingdom across the sea, where the King resides, from the kingdom in which Leinad, his father, and the rest of the people live. What does the Great Sea represent?

3. Peyton tells Leinad at the end of chapter 1, "No matter what a man's occupation, he must be ready to fight for the King. One never knows if he will be called upon to serve the King in battle." How are you preparing yourself for service to God in this ultimate battle between Good and Evil?

CHAPTER 2

1. In chapter 2, the character of Gabrik is introduced. Who does he represent?

2. Many of the names within the Kingdom Series are formed from arranged words and letters derived from representative words. What words were used to form *Arrethtrae*?

3. Gabrik responds to Leinad's question about the sword with these words: "The sword is for one who is willing to serve the King...and the people." What does this foreshadow?

# DISCUSSION QUESTIONS

CHAPTER 3

1. In this chapter we learn that Peyton and Dinan were chosen by the King to establish a new kingdom in Arrethtrae. What does this part of the story represent?

2. Why does Peyton feel responsible for the destruction of the new kingdom when it was Dinan who accepted the gift from Lord Sinjon?

3. Leinad and Peyton discuss the training Leinad received from his father, and Peyton asks Leinad which of the teachings was most important. Leinad responds, "To be loyal to the King, even unto death, and to have compassion for my fellow man." This statement is the heart of the Code; what does it represent?

4. We learn that the King doesn't want to rule over Arrethtrae by force, but wants the kingdom to submit out of the people's own desire. This symbolizes a very important aspect of God's character. What is it, and why is it important to know this?

5. Leinad realizes that his father trained him carefully and purposefully. Can you think of times in your life when God was training or teaching you for a specific purpose?

CHAPTER 4

1. In chapter 4, Leinad is captured by an enemy army but is given the opportunity to fight with a scarred man. Who does this man represent?

2. At the end of the chapter, Gabrik says the hope still lives on even though Peyton is dead. What does this mean, and what does it represent?

3. Leinad and Zane fight in this chapter. Because of Leinad's extensive training with the sword, he is able to survive

the fight. Christians often experience trials because of their faith. Have you ever felt that you were at odds with the world because of your faith in Jesus Christ?

CHAPTER 5

1. Leinad asks Gabrik, "What is the promise and where do I find it?" This is the key question in *Kingdom's Dawn* and *Kingdom's Hope*. What is the promise?

2. Leinad's first assignment from the King is to warn the people of Mankin about the Vactor Deluge and to help them flee to safety. What does the Vactor Deluge symbolize, and who does Leinad represent here?

CHAPTER 6

1. Leinad and Tess ride Deliverance to safety in the Tara Hills Mountain Range. What does Deliverance represent?

2. Leinad becomes very discouraged when the people of Mankin ignore his warning. Only when Tess speaks words of encouragement does Leinad remember his responsibility to Tess and to the King. Can you think of a time in your life when a brother or sister in Christ encouraged you? Try to be a Tess to someone you know.

CHAPTER 7

1. In this chapter we are introduced to "a man from a distant land" who saves Leinad and Tess from starvation. Who do you think this man is? Who do you think he represents?

2. Who does Leinad represent in this chapter, and why do you think so?

3. The man from a distant land gives Leinad his next assignment from the King: He and Tess must travel to the Valley of Nan. Why doesn't Leinad doubt this man?

# DISCUSSION QUESTIONS

## CHAPTER 8

1. In this chapter, the biblical character Leinad symbolizes changes again. Who is he now?

2. Leinad despairs and doubts that the King is truly powerful enough to rule over Arrethtrae. He questions whether his misfortune is a part of the King's plan. Not until later in the book do we see that it really was in the King's plan for Leinad to go to Nyland. Have you ever felt that God wasn't big enough to be in control of your life? Find passages to help you remember that God is good, just, powerful, and always in control.

## CHAPTER 9

1. Tess survived an attack by vicious raiders, later identified as Eminafs, who had no purpose other than to "kill people and steal things." What do the Eminafs represent? (Hint: Rearrange the letters.)

2. Although she becomes a slave, Tess is preserved because she flees the destruction of the Eminafs. At this point in the story, what biblical group of people does Tess represent?

## CHAPTER 10

1. During their duel, Leinad impresses Fairos with his swordsmanship. What biblical event does this portray?

2. When Fairos orders Leinad to kneel and swear his allegiance, Leinad refuses because he already serves the King. Leinad recognized that "no one can serve two masters" (Matthew 6:24). Is there anything in your life that demands your time and energy and diminishes your devotion to God?

CHAPTER 11

1. In this chapter Leinad trains Fairos's guards using his skill as a swordsman. Later, Fairos and his guards are victorious in their battle against the Eminafs. What do these two events represent?

2. Leinad tries to warn the people from the Valley of Nan about Fairos's intentions. Once again, the very people he's trying to save are apathetic about his warnings. Because of this, they are enslaved by Fairos. Have you ever ignored the godly counsel of a friend or a parent? What happened?

CHAPTER 12

1. In this chapter, Leinad's biblical character representation changes. Who does he symbolize, and how do you know this? Find specific passages in the Bible that the allegory is based on.

2. Leinad becomes angry when he sees a fellow slave being tormented by a guard. The Bible has a verse regarding righteous anger; find that passage. Have you ever experienced righteous anger? If so, what were you angry about?

CHAPTER 13

1. In this chapter, Leinad is left to die in the Banteen Desert. What does this event represent?

2. Leinad tries to loosen the straps that keep him chained to the desert floor, but only succeeds in creating small cracks around each stake. Later on in the chapter there is a thunderstorm that not only frightens the Moshi Beasts from killing Leinad, but causes rain to pour into the small cracks, loosening the stakes. Sometimes it feels as if we are at the end of our rope, but if we call

out to God, as Leinad called to the King, God will provide a way to save us. Find passages in the Bible that refer to His promise to listen if we call to Him.

CHAPTER 14

1. In this chapter, Leinad comes face-to-face with the King, and it is a turning point in Leinad's life. This event is allegorical to a specific event in the Bible regarding Moses. What is that event?

2. The King gives Leinad an arduous task: to free the people of Nan from their enslavement in Nyland. However, Leinad offers excuses because he doubts his ability to accomplish the task. This represents when Moses argued with God in Exodus 3 and 4. When God gives us tasks, sometimes it feels as if we are unworthy of the trust He puts in us. Have you ever given God excuses when He told you to do something?

3. In this chapter, the King continues Leinad's training with the sword, saying, "What your father began, I shall complete." What might this statement mean for you personally?

4. The King warns Leinad of his worst enemy. Who is Leinad's worst enemy and why? Can you find Bible verses that pertain to this?

5. In the final passages of the chapter, the King knights Leinad "in the harsh landscape of the desert, the only place where a man truly begins to understand his purpose in life." Not only does this represent when God chooses Moses after his self-reflection in the desert, but it also applies to each of us. Thinking back in your life, when did you learn the most? Was it during a time of trial or of ease?

# ANSWERS TO
# DISCUSSION QUESTIONS

CHAPTER 1

1. The sword represents the Word of God. Hebrews 4:12 says, "For the word of God is living and powerful, and sharper than any two-edged sword, piercing even to the division of soul and spirit, and of joints and marrow, and is a discerner of the thoughts and intents of the heart." Leinad questions his training because everyone questions his or her purpose in life and the authenticity of faith at some point. Through prayer, wise counsel, and training, the truth of God's Word is revealed.

2. The gulf between the spiritual world of heaven and the physical world of earth.

3. One way we can prepare is to study God's Word and develop a close, personal relationship with Him. Second Timothy 2:15 states, "Be diligent to present yourself approved to God, a worker who does not need to be ashamed, rightly dividing the word of truth." Also, Ephesians 6: 11–17 defines the battle against spiritual darkness and encourages us to "put on the whole armor of God."

CHAPTER 2

1. Specifically, Gabrik represents the messenger angel Gabriel. However, Gabrik is also used to represent other angelic beings throughout the first two books.

2. *Terra* and *Earth*. Also, take a close look at *Leinad*.

3. Leinad's symbolic calling as a prophet to be an instrument through which God talks to, leads, and guides His people.

# ANSWERS TO DISCUSSION QUESTIONS

CHAPTER 3

1. This represents the Creation, Adam and Eve, and the Fall of mankind through sin in the Garden of Eden (Genesis 1–3).

2. As the husband, Peyton had a responsibility to protect his wife (Genesis 3:16).

3. The two great commandments as stated by Jesus in Matthew 22:37–40: Jesus said to him, "'You shall love the Lord your God with all your heart, with all your soul, and with all your mind.' This is the first and great commandment. And the second is like it: 'You shall love your neighbor as yourself.' On these two commandments hang all the Law and the Prophets."

4. This symbolizes our free will and God's desire that we choose to serve Him. It is important to know this because it reveals part of God's nature: He loves us, but He will not violate the free will He gave us in order to have a relationship with us.

5. Answer based on personal experience.

CHAPTER 4

1. Cain (Genesis 4:15b).

2. This means that the hope of the coming Prince still remains and that the one chosen to deliver this message of hope is still alive. Although God's children may be martyred for their faith, the message of truth (that Christ is coming again) will never be lost.

3. Answer based on personal experience.

CHAPTER 5

1. The promise is revealed in the next book, *Kingdom's Hope*.

2. The Vactor Deluge is the Great Flood, and Leinad represents Noah. Simultaneously, Tess represents Noah's family, the faithful few who believed Noah in spite of all the ridicule (Genesis 6:13–22).

CHAPTER 6

1. The ark (Genesis 7:1).

2. Answer based on personal experience.

CHAPTER 7

1. In the Kingdom Series, this man is the Prince, and allegorically he is the preincarnate Christ.

2. Leinad now represents Abraham. Abraham means "the friend of God."

3. Leinad recognized the mark of the King on the man's sword.

CHAPTER 8

1. Joseph.

2. 2 Timothy 4:18; James 4:10; Psalms 46:10; Isaiah 55:8–9; Jeremiah 32:17; Nahum 1:7.

CHAPTER 9

1. The Eminafs represent the famine in Egypt and the surrounding regions, including Canaan.

2. Tess represents the children of Israel who go to Egypt to find food.

CHAPTER 10

1. This represents Joseph's interpretation of Pharaoh's dream.

2. Answer based on personal experience.

# ANSWERS TO DISCUSSION QUESTIONS

## CHAPTER 11

1. God gave Joseph the interpretation of Pharaoh's dream so that Egypt was prepared for the famine. As a result, Joseph was given the responsibility to store food during the seven years of plenty to prepare for the seven years of famine. Likewise, Leinad's training prepared Fairos's men for the battle against the Eminafs.

2. Answer based on personal experience.

## CHAPTER 12

1. Leinad now represents Moses (Exodus 2:11–12).

2. Ephesians 4:26: "'Be angry, and do not sin': do not let the sun go down on your wrath."

## CHAPTER 13

1. Moses living in the wilderness after his exile from Egypt.

2. 2 Chronicles 7:14; Psalm 50:15; 55:16; 86:7; 91:15; 116:2; Jeremiah 29:12; 33:3.

## CHAPTER 14

1. Moses and the burning bush.

2. Answer based on personal experience.

3. Answer based on personal experience.

4. The King warns Leinad of himself. The King continues by telling Leinad that if he becomes arrogant in his skill with the sword, he will fall. In the same way, God hates pride in His children and has warned us through these following passages: Psalm 119:21; 138:6; Proverbs 6:17; 16:5; 16:18; 21:4; Isaiah 13:11; Luke 1:51; James 4:6; 1 John 2:16.

5. Answer based on personal experience.

# Expedition
### Written for Kingdom's Dawn

Music by Emily Elizabeth Black
Lyrics by Chuck Black
Edited by Brittney Dyanne Black

On a jour-ney thru the wil-der-ness, expe-di-tion of the faith-ful & bold, I will search out truth & righ-teous-ness & to my heart will hold. On to the pro-mised land, I am search-ing for the kingdom of the heart. Who will de-liv-er me? Oh, King of the land and of the sea. O'r the moun-tains, through the val-ley low, 'cross the plains and near the

# AUTHOR'S COMMENTARY

The Old Testament tells the story of mankind from its beginning to the dawn of a redeemer…a deliverer. Its pages reveal to the world the promise that someday One would come who could defeat the evil one. If the Old Testament was categorized as a drama, it would be classified as a tragedy. However, it is a tragedy that ends with hope and a promise. Although the Jews have endured tremendous trials and persecution, it is through these chosen people that this hope and promise came from God.

Divine wisdom made manifest the need for a Savior. God granted this wisdom to a select few men who were consumed with the zeal of the Holy Spirit. It was their mission in life to reveal God's will to His chosen people, the Jews. These men were respected, feared, and persecuted for this throughout Bible history. Ultimately they brought the message of a Savior who would redeem mankind and eventually usher in an age of peace and prosperity.

*Kingdom's Dawn* is the beginning of an allegorical novel series that attempts to capture this incredible true story of the Bible. The prologue and epilogue are given by a man named Cedric as he looks back to the time of his mentor,

Leinad. Later, in *Kingdom's Edge,* more is revealed about Cedric and his important role. Suffice it to say that the entire Kingdom Series is told by him. *Kingdom's Dawn* and *Kingdom's Hope* are told by Cedric from a third person account as he passes along the story Leinad (and also Tess) told him. But *Kingdom's Edge* is told from Cedric's point of view as he gives us a firsthand account of the events recorded there. Cedric represents all of the believers in our Lord and Savior Jesus Christ from the time of Peter up to the present.

The central character in *Kingdom's Dawn* is Cedric's wise old mentor, Leinad, when he was a young man. He represents all the select men who were instrumental in revealing God's message to the people either through their lives, their dreams, or direct revelation. Through the development of the novel, you can see many of the biblical characters that Leinad represents. Some include Seth, Noah, Abraham, Joseph, and Moses. In the next novel, *Kingdom's Hope,* Leinad represents most of the Old Testament prophets.

The sword throughout the Kingdom Series represents the Word of God. The challenge in *Kingdom's Dawn* was differentiating between the real swords used in the Old Testament battles and the "Word of God" sword used by the prophets to reveal God's will to the people. Extreme care was taken to create allegorical content centered on the sword that directly symbolized God's Word through the prophets. For example, God gave Joseph the interpretation of Pharaoh's dream that allowed him to store up food for the forthcoming famine, which ultimately strengthened Pharaoh's rule. Allegorically, it was Leinad's skill with the sword that saved Nyland from the Eminafs and increased Fairos's rule.

Tess represents the faithful remnant that stayed true to the Lord and did not abandon the prophets even when the rest of the nation turned its back on them. One could speculate that there was a special understanding and relationship between the faithful and the prophets. In this novel, Tess represents Enoch, Noah's family, Joshua, Caleb, and many more.

The evil forces of the Dark Knight are obviously Satan and his fallen angels. Zane represents the unrepentant mass of mankind that begins with Cain and carries through to the evil people at the time of Noah's flood and beyond.

A discerning mind will see many significant biblical events allegorically portrayed, such as the Creation, Paradise, the Fall, the Flood, and the four hundred years of captivity in Egypt. *Kingdom's Hope* continues this line of symbolism to the end of the Old Testament.

My hope and prayer is that your reading of this novel will inspire you to explore the infallible Word of God as you investigate the incredible journey of mankind and our arrival at the realization that we all desperately need a savior...*the* Savior, Jesus!

*The LORD is my rock and my fortress and my deliverer;*
*My God, my strength, in whom I will trust;*
*My shield and the horn of my salvation, my stronghold.*
PSALM 18:2